A TIME TO RUN

When nurse Lynn Crane finds employment at an isolated manor house in the Yorkshire countryside, all is not what it seems. As she nurses her attractive patient, Serge Varda, Prince of Estavia, an alarming truth emerges: her employers, Max Ozerov and the sinister Dr Miros, his countrymen, plan to wrest control of the country from him. The young couple escape from almost certain death, but, as Serge is eventually restored to state duties, will he share them with Lynne?

Books by Janet Whitehead
in the Linford Romance Library:

FAR EASTERN PROMISE

JANET WHITEHEAD

A TIME
TO RUN

Complete and Unabridged

LINFORD
Leicester

First published in Great Britain in 1996

First Linford Edition
published 2007

British Library CIP Data

Whitehead, Janet
    A time to run.—Large print ed.—
Linford romance library
    1. Love stories
    2. Large type books
    I. Title
    823.9'14 [F]

    ISBN 978–1–84617–875–7

Published by
F. A. Thorpe (Publishing)
Anstey, Leicestershire

Set by Words & Graphics Ltd.
Anstey, Leicestershire
Printed and bound in Great Britain by
T. J. International Ltd., Padstow, Cornwall

This book is printed on acid-free paper

1

Much later, Lynn Crane would remember how innocently it had all started and, in her darkest moments, before it was all finally resolved, she would bitterly regret her involvement in it . . . And yet in another way she would thank her lucky stars, too. For, while the days that followed brought danger and intrigue, they brought something else besides, something altogether more gentle and loving, something far more meaningful and permanent to what had previously been a rather unloved life.

Yes, it had all started so innocently, with nothing more sinister than a job interview in a sprawling, fortified manor house set amidst gently-rolling hills several miles outside the city of York . . .

'Well, Miss Crane,' Max Ozerov had said.

He was a tall, angular man seated across from her at the large desk in the centre of the richly-appointed drawing-room-cum-office. He closed a manilla folder before him and brought his eyes up to her face. He had very dark, brown eyes, magnified by small, thick lenses with practically invisible frames, and he wore his blond-going-on-grey hair in a severe Teutonic crop.

Lynn had looked at him enquiringly. He was an administrator or official of some kind; she realised afterwards that he had kept his own part in what followed deliberately vague. He looked to be about forty or so, and was rather formal and correct. He was proud of his country, a former USSR state now independent, and a map of the country occupied pride of place on the wall to their right. He had made no secret of that, although, as she was later to learn, he was a man of many secrets.

'I certainly cannot fault your nursing qualifications,' he said in lightly- accented English. 'And your previous employers speak highly of you. Yes, in all respects, I find you most suitable for the post. But I am afraid I have one or two more questions to ask before you may consider the job yours.'

Lynn offered an indulgent smile that she hoped masked her discomfort. She was a slender, graceful girl in her mid-twenties, dressed smartly in a lightweight, burgundy suit and an open-necked, white, cotton blouse. She looked every inch a confident, go-ahead career woman, and it was true that she certainly had confidence in her abilities.

But the large, imposing house, the heavy security she had encountered at the half-timbered gatehouse outside — she had been prepared for none of it, and it had intimidated her somewhat, thrown her off-balance.

'You come from a large family?' he asked suddenly.

The question surprised her and she raised one fine eyebrow quizzically before responding.

'Well, yes,' she replied after a

moment. 'Yes and no, really.'

'Oh?'

She shifted uncomfortably in her chair, never truly at ease when discussing the subject that confronted her now. Taking a deep breath, she said, 'Well, as near as I've been able to piece it together, I do come from a large family. I was the youngest of six children. Unfortunately, my father died in an accident about two months before I was born and — well, the way it was explained to me afterwards, my mother found herself in such serious financial difficulties that it was decided that I should be put up for adoption.'

'Very sad,' Max Ozerov said, without noticeable compassion. 'You never traced your real mother?'

'I tried, but I was too late. She was already dead by that time, and my brothers and sisters — well, you know how it can be sometimes. They just drifted apart.'

He considered that, then fired a supplementary question at her.

'And your adoptive parents?'

'I spent most of my early years in and out of foster homes,' Lynn replied.

His line of questioning puzzled her. She should have known then that something about the situation was wrong, but as he had already pointed out, she was a fully-qualified nurse and eager to make her way in her chosen profession. Although she had worked off and on for an agency, she had discovered this vacancy for herself, tucked away in a personal column, and sensing that it might be a stepping-stone to higher things, she was now answering Mr Ozerov's questions as honestly as she could, hoping for the best.

'I'm afraid I was quite a sickly child, although, as you can see, I've grown out of all that now. At the time, however, I don't think potential parents ever saw me as much of a catch.'

'So you have no strong familial connections?' he pressed.

'No.'

'And no — romantic attachments?'

'Not at the moment.'

'And you live alone?'

Frowning, Lynn said, 'Excuse me, Mr Ozerov, but may I ask what all this has to do with the job I'm applying for?'

His smile was conciliatory as he sat back, took off his glasses and peered through them, checking that the lenses were thoroughly without blemish or smear.

'I am sorry if my line of questioning appears too personal, but I have my reasons, I assure you. As I intimated to you at the start of this interview, the successful candidate will be occupying a position of great trust. Without going into too much detail at this stage, there is a question of security to be considered. Also, you will be required to live in, should we decide to offer you the job. A family, or boyfriend, or even a flat-mate, might object to that, as indeed you might yourself. I am only trying to ensure — '

6

Somewhat mollified by his explanation, Lynn settled back and gave him another smile of her own.

'I'm sorry. Of course, I should have realised.'

'And I should have explained myself more clearly at the outset,' he responded. He put his glasses back on and leaned forward with his elbows on the table's edge, his fingers interlaced in an arch beneath his chin. The girl before him was attractive, with well-spaced, blue eyes, a straight, firm nose and heart-shaped lips above a small, pert chin. She wore her natural, blonde hair pulled back from her face and tied with a simple clasp.

'I am curious, Miss Crane,' he said, 'as to how you come to speak Russian?'

Lynn felt her nerves settling at last.

'Oh,' she replied, 'the answer to that is simple. I shared lodgings with a Russian girl at nursing college. I helped her to improve her English and in return she taught me enough Russian to just about hold my own in a conversation.'

'Excellent, excellent,' he said with obvious approval. With a sigh he sat back again. 'Well, I must say, you have impressed me on all counts. You would appear to be exactly the candidate we have been looking for.'

She was pleased. 'Does that mean — ' she began.

He glanced sideways at her. 'That you have the job?' he finished.

He paused a moment, then, reaching a decision, he nodded emphatically.

'Yes, Miss — Nurse Crane. Yes, it does.'

'Thank you.'

He took a sheet of paper from the folder, scanned it and handed it to her.

'You will be required to sign a declaration of confidence, of course. It is a purely routine formality, but I'm sure you understand.'

'Of course. When — ah, when will you want me to take up the position?'

He looked at her sharply. 'Why, immediately,' he replied, as if the answer should have been obvious.

'Oh . . . '

'Yes? There is a problem?'

Not wishing to appear awkward, she tried to make light of it.

'It's just that — well, I didn't take anything with me, any of my clothes or personal items.'

'I will arrange for someone to collect some things from your flat in London,' he replied. 'By tonight, your quarters here will be a — what is the expression, a home from home. That would be agreeable?'

Not especially liking the idea, but wanting the job very much, Lynn nodded.

'Yes, it — it's very kind of you.'

'Not at all,' he replied, indicating the declaration that still lay on the table.

Lynn quickly read through the form, which was printed in English. As her new employer had told her, it was simply an affirmation similar to that of the Official Secrets Act, which many people were required to sign even though they seldom if ever came into contact with sensitive or secret information. Mr Ozerov offered her his pen and she signed her name in a series of confident strokes.

'We have already discussed salary,' he reminded her. 'I take it you find our terms generous?'

'Very.'

'Good. Of course, we can only offer you a short-term contract at this stage. We do not anticipate that your services will be required for much more than a fortnight. A month at the most, but if you pass this probationary period with distinction, there is no reason why we should not make you part of our permanent medical staff eventually.'

'Well, I'll certainly do the best I can.'

'I'm sure you will.' He rose abruptly, took back his pen and slotted it into his breast pocket. 'I will take you to see your patient now,' he said. 'His personal physician, Dr Miros, will explain his illness, and the nature of your duties, more fully. Later I will have my secretary show you to your room. I am sure you will find everything to your satisfaction.'

He came around the desk towards her. He was wearing a dark grey, slightly old-fashioned suit that hung on his spare frame. He shepherded her from the office and down a long, opulent corridor, making idle conversation as they weaved through the vast, ancient brown-brick house. Lynn made all the right noises in response to his somewhat over-polite monologue, but inside she was experiencing the first of several misgivings.

She had not counted on starting work immediately. There were still people to tell of her prolonged absence, even if she didn't have a family, a boyfriend or a flat-mate. And she certainly didn't care for the idea of someone else going to her flat and collecting her belongings.

However, she was committed now. She had been intrigued by the small, inconspicuous advert to which she had applied. She'd gone for the job because it had piqued her curiosity and would look good on her references, if she got it. Now that she was actually here, though, in this large, brooding house, in this isolated part of the Yorkshire countryside, to all intents and purposes shut off from the rest of the world . . .

Yes, she thought, I feel like I'm a prisoner.

Almost at once she dispelled the thought. It was ridiculous, and it reflected her naïveté and basic lack of experience. She was twenty-five. It was about time she broadened that experience. And this, she told herself resolutely, was as good a way as any to start.

They started up a wide staircase, past ancient works of art in ornate, gilt frames.

'May I ask the name of the patient?' Lynn asked.

Mr Ozerov glanced at her. 'You may,' he replied, 'but I am afraid I cannot tell you. To you he will simply be . . . ' He thought for a moment, then said with a smile, 'Mr X.'

'Oh. Security again, I take it?'

'I'm afraid so. Tiresome, but necessary.'

They reached the top of the staircase and turned right, down another long hallway, their footsteps clicking against highly-polished parquet flooring, their passage flanked alternately by suits of armour, long windows draped with sunshine-filled lace curtains and yet more paintings.

At last they stopped at a door midway along the hall and Lynn's companion rapped his knuckles against one panel, then entered. They found themselves in a large room with a high ceiling and two big windows which offered a breathtaking view of the grounds in which the house was set. Gently-rolling hills were stippled with orderly rows of hazel trees and fields sprinkled with cheerful yellow daffodils and nodding bluebells.

The room itself was painted in restful shades of blue and white, stripped of all furniture save for a desk, two chairs, a filing cabinet, an examination couch and some other medical paraphernalia that was just visible behind a partly-extended modesty screen.

A dark-skinned man with raven-black hair sweeping back from a high forehead had been sitting behind the desk. Now he rose to his feet. He was tall, in his early thirties, athletically built and wearing a finely-tailored, navy-blue suit, a startlingly white shirt and a maroon tie. He came around the desk and smiled at Mr Ozerov, revealing even teeth.

'Ah, Doctor,' Ozerov said, 'I've brought your new nurse to see the patient, whom we have just agreed to call Mr X.'

Irrationally, Lynn found herself thinking, I never agreed to any such thing.

Ozerov went on, 'Doctor Miros, meet Nurse Lynn Crane. Nurse Crane, it is my pleasure to introduce Dr Vitale Miros, one of our finest physicians.'

'Ah, you are too generous with your

praise, Max,' Dr Miros said. He took Lynn's hand, held it for a moment, then released it. He had a very cool, soft palm, she noticed. 'How do you do, Nurse Crane? I'm sure we will enjoy working together.'

'I hope so.'

Mr Ozerov took that as his cue to leave.

'I will allow you to explain Nurse Crane's duties,' he said. Then, turning to Lynn, he added, 'If I may just trouble you for the keys of your flat . . .'

She looked at him, feeling another pang of reluctance, but fished in her bag for her keys. When she tried to detach her front-door key from the ring, however, he simply reached out and took the whole thing, and when she automatically held on to it, he explained easily, 'If I take your car keys as well, I can have one of the staff drive your car around to the garages at the rear of the house.'

Well, that made sense, she supposed,

and surrendered the key-ring without further argument, telling herself she was being immature and over-imaginative, that she should loosen up and become more flexible.

Ozerov gave her another smile — he was all smiles — then turned and left the room.

'I expect you find this all rather daunting?' Dr Miros said, breaking the silence.

She turned back to him and admitted ruefully, 'I do, just a bit.'

'Don't. Although you will probably find that you are kept in the dark about many things during your stay here, always remember that you're not the only one. None of us is told any more than we need to know. It's safer that way.'

'Safer?' she asked uncertainly.

He waved a hand. 'Please, don't let me alarm you. I am sworn to secrecy, just like everyone else, but I will tell you this much — as soon as you get used to the high security we have to endure, all of this will become just like any other job to you.'

'I hope so,' Lynn said. 'May I see the patient now?'

Dr Miros shrugged his broad shoulders. 'Why not?'

He indicated that she should follow him across the room to a door in the facing wall. When they got there, he produced a key and unlocked the door. This seemed to Lynn to be a rather unusual procedure, unless of course the patient had contracted a contagious disease and thus had to be kept in isolation.

He pushed the door open just then, interrupting her train of thought, and allowed her to go through ahead of him. Lynn stepped into another, slightly smaller, blue room with an equally high ceiling. Looking around, she noticed that it was even more sparsely appointed than the outer office. A bed projected from the wall beside the single window, and beside that sat a small cabinet upon which had been set out an assortment of medications and a carafe of water.

In the bed lay a young man.

At once he claimed Lynn's attention, and she walked slowly to the foot of the bed so that she could study him better.

He was in a deep, drug-induced slumber, his broad chest rising and falling sluggishly beneath the crisp, white sheets. Lynn listened to the sounds of his heavy, laboured breathing, and frowned. A light sheen of perspiration glistened on his forehead, and immediately, she took a paper towel from a box on the cabinet and gently blotted it away.

All of her own doubts and misgivings vanished as she looked at him. Under any other circumstances, he would have commanded her attention for a much different reason. He was tall and of a muscular build, of a similar age to her own. In other, healthier times, he would no doubt have had a ruddy tan, but now his well-proportioned face was pale and a little wasted.

Lynn's clear, blue eyes roved across his features, noting the thick, blue-black spill of his hair, the smooth forehead sloping down to thickish brows, eyelids now closed down so that his lashes formed two gentle U shapes above high, pronounced cheekbones. His nose was short and straight, his lips a pale pink, slightly parted now in a troubled, incoherent murmuring.

Lynn looked at him, along his surprisingly rugged jawline, and muttered absently, 'Who is he?'

Dr Miros appeared magically at her side. He had moved so quietly that she gave a little gasp of surprise.

'He is Mr X,' he replied. 'Remember?'

She nodded. 'Yes. Of course.' She looked down at the young man again. 'What's wrong with him?'

'Malaria.'

She echoed the word. 'Malaria?'

Dr Miros nodded and went to look out of the window, as if the patient were no longer of any particular interest to him.

'Yes. He acquired it on a state visit when he was just a boy.'

Lynn opened her mouth to speak but quickly fell silent again. The voice in her mind repeated what the doctor had said, however. Malaria he had contracted on a state visit. She returned a compassionate gaze to the attractive, unconscious man in the bed. Was he royalty, then, she wondered.

'What medication is he on?'

'A mixture of quinine, pyrimethamine and one of the sulphones,' Miros replied.

'Administered intramuscularly?'

'Orally.' He gestured to the foot of the bed. 'It's all there on his chart. You can read up on it before you begin.'

'Very good, Doctor.'

Coming back over, he said, 'So, there you have it. All quite routine, yes?'

'Yes, Doctor.'

'Your duties will be to ensure that Mr X here receives his medication on time, and to be available should he wake up and require help. We will share this work on a rota system.'

'I understand.'

'Now, if you will excuse me for just a moment,' Miros said, 'I will go and ring for Mr Ozerov's secretary to come and show you to your quarters. Once you've settled in, you can commence your duties . . .'

Mr Ozerov's secretary turned out to be a short, bulky woman in her late forties, with blonde hair worn in a taut bun at the back of her head and a flat, largely inexpressive face. Her name was Yasha Schulmann. She collected Lynn from Dr Miros' office and then took her on another seemingly endless trek through the house until they reached Lynn's quarters.

'Here,' she said in halting English when they finally reached their destination. 'Is yours.'

Lynn decided to practise some of her Russian, which had grown rusty — to say the least — from long disuse. 'Thank you, Yasha.'

Surprise showed in the secretary's otherwise flinty, brown eyes.

'You speak Russian?' she asked in her own tongue.

'A little,' Lynn replied self-consciously. 'And very slowly, I'm afraid, but if you're patient with me, I hope I'll become more fluent.'

The bulky little woman inclined her head, then gestured to the room into which they had come. It had been furnished as a comfortable sitting-room, with a sofa, a nest of tables, a television and a bookcase that held an assortment of paperbacks and magazines. It had been tastefully decorated in shades of pastel pink and lavender.

'You like?' the secretary enquired.

'Why, yes, it's — '

Yasha brushed past her and briskly opened doors, her manner brusque and businesslike. 'The bedroom is here, the bathroom here. Staff dine in the kitchen. I will come and fetch you when it is time. Or, if you prefer, I can arrange to have your meals sent up to you.'

'Thank you.'

Lynn looked around in some disbelief. Her quarters more closely resembled the finest suite that money could buy, in the plushest hotel in the world. The bedroom was startling, with a huge bed and soft, silk pillows that more closely resembled oversized marshmallows. The furniture was delicate and white, and the en suite bathroom was equally grand.

She turned back to the secretary and said, 'Are you — '

But Yasha was stalking out already, closing the door behind her with a soft click.

Without warning Lynn felt her sense of isolation returning, and even the most luxurious surroundings could do little to combat that. Setting her handbag down on a padded chair just inside the bedroom, she crossed to the bed. A starched, white, cotton uniform had been laid out for her on the bed. She checked the label and found it to be her size.

With nothing better to do, she decided to change into it and then return to her patient. She was only going to be here for a fortnight, a month at the most, which was about the longest a recurring bout of malaria tended to run. She might as well try to settle in as quickly as she could and make sure that her mysterious charge made a full and speedy recovery. Then she could leave this unfriendly, secretive place.

Just as she was taking off her jacket, she heard the growl of a car engine drifting in from the courtyard below the window. It had a peculiar sound that was instantly familiar to her.

She went over and looked out. She had parked her car to one side of the house upon her arrival. Now, she realised that her room must occupy a wing that overlooked it. As a member of staff drove the car away, presumably so that it could be parked out of sight in one of the garages, she only felt her sense of loneliness growing more acute.

She was annoyed with herself. No-one had forced her to apply for this job, after all. She had come of her own free will. Just because it looked as if it were going to be something out of the ordinary for her, there was no reason to start yearning for home and familiarity.

In any case, she told herself irritably, what was home, anyway? A less than pleasing flat in a less than pleasing part of a noisy, overcrowded city? That wasn't strictly true, of course, but she was exaggerating her situation in order to put things here into a clearer perspective.

Again she turned her attention to the window and the rolling, thickly-grassed fields and hills in which the house was nestled. If anything, she should be congratulating herself on getting such a prestigious post, and making the most of it while she could.

She began to feel a little better after that, and returned to the bed, where she slipped off her blouse. Within moments she had changed into her uniform. Checking herself briefly in the full-length mirror behind the bedroom door, she smoothed the crisp material with her palms, decided she would pass muster, and then retraced her steps to Dr Miros' office.

2

Lynn spent the remainder of the day monitoring her patient, who continued to punctuate his drug-induced sleep every so often with the odd murmur or groan.

After a while she attuned herself to the rhythm of his deep breathing, as had always been her custom, so that she would be alerted to even the slightest change within moments of it occurring.

The afternoon passed slowly. Shortly after her return to Dr Miros' office, the doctor had excused himself. After he left, she saw no-one else. Around them the big house was oppressively silent. Lynn regularly wiped the young man's sweaty face and checked his temperature, which was only marginally above normal.

Some time later, she set about familiarising herself with the impromptu surgery and everything she might be likely to need.

The day was bright and pleasantly warm. She went over to the window, intending to look out at the magnificent view, but as she approached it, she realised that the window was barred.

She frowned, momentarily perplexed. More security? It seemed likely.

The thought made her glance almost guiltily around the room, searching for other security devices, such as hidden cameras. She didn't find any, but the idea that she might be under some form of surveillance made her go cold, and she quickly rubbed her bare arms to rid them of goosebumps.

Her patient — she refused to think of him by the faintly mocking name that Mr Ozerov had given him — moaned softly and stirred in his sleep. Lynn went over to him and studied him with curiosity.

Who are you, she thought. Someone important, that was certain. Why else would there be so much emphasis on security here? According to his chart, he had been in the grip of his recurring malaria for several days now. The dark shading of bristles along his firm jaw and above his lips confirmed as much.

She noticed his frown and wondered what tortured dreams were flitting through his delirious mind.

It was then that she realised he had woken up and was looking at her.

She bent over him and wiped his slick face. He watched her through glazed, fever-wracked, smoke-grey eyes, too weak to lift his head from the pillow, just about managing to work his lips although forming actual words seemed to be beyond him. His eyes continued to move over her. They were crowded with confusion. Again he tried to speak, but again he failed.

Quickly searching her memory for the right words, Lynn said gently in Russian, 'There, there, relax now. You're all right.'

She wished she knew his name, because sometimes just the use of a person's name was enough to convince them that you meant them no harm, that you were a friend, that you could be trusted to look after them.

His hands stirred beneath the bed-sheets, making a soft, rustling sound. With great effort he managed to drag one long-fingered hand out into the open and grab her wrist. She took his hand in one of her own and gently prised it loose. Immediately his fingers tightened around hers with surprising strength, and he tried to speak again, but his throat only made a dry, clicking sound.

'Would you like a drink?' she asked, still speaking Russian.

It was vital that he replace the fluids he was losing, otherwise dehydration would become a very real threat.

Slowly he nodded.

She extricated herself from his grip and poured water from the carafe on the bedside cabinet, then came around to the other side of the bed, gently helping to raise his head with one hand

and holding the glass to his lips with the other.

He managed a couple of swallows, but the effort seemed to exhaust him and she allowed him to rest. She checked his temperature — still normal — and took his pulse, the wild racing of which confirmed his obvious agitation.

Methodically she checked him for any skin rashes, retinal damage or hair loss, all three of which could be side-effects of the anti-malarial drugs, and he watched her silently as she went about her business.

Speaking softly, she asked, 'Do you have a headache?'

It took him a long time to understand the question, but when he did he shook his head.

Holding one hand up in front of his face, she said, 'Follow my finger.'

Slowly she moved it back and forth, up and down.

His clouded, grey eyes tracked it with some small effort, but not enough to indicate any blurred vision.

As she lowered her hand again, he suddenly reached for it, moving with unexpected speed. Again he fastened his fingers on hers, tightening the grip in order to communicate some of his urgency to her. She watched as he struggled to speak, her face wincing at the huge effort he was making. Finally, after several long, frantic moments, a croak emerged from his throat.

'Who . . . ?'

'I'm Lynn,' she explained. 'Lynn Crane. Your nurse.'

His eyes travelled across her face again, down over the uniform, back up to her face. His dark, thickish brows met slightly over the bridge of his nose as he tried to make sense of what, to him, must be a nonsensical situation. Again his mouth worked with effort.

'What . . . ? Where . . . ?'

'You've got malaria,' she explained, speaking as clearly and slowly as she could so that he would be able to follow her. 'But you're safe now. We're looking after you. You'll soon be well again.'

'Malaria?'

She nodded. 'Rest now. Sleep.' Again she wished she knew his name. 'You need lots of sleep.'

He shook his head weakly. 'No — no — I must get out . . . '

He tried to rise, but in his weakened state she was able to restrain him with ease. She checked the time. His next medication was due. She prepared the tablets, made him open his mouth, take them and wash them down with another sip of water.

Almost at once his eyes blurred and although he tried to fight it, he began a quick descent back into unconsciousness. Just before it consumed him completely, however, he muttered something under his breath that she didn't quite catch. She leaned over him, straining her ears to make sense of his desperate, panting whisperings . . .

At last he began to breath deeply again.

'Any problems here, Nurse Crane?'

'Oh!' She turned quickly, catching the breath in her throat.

Dr Miros came farther into the room and closed the door behind him. His eyes came up from the patient in the bed to the nurse standing beside him, and he smiled disarmingly.

'I'm sorry if I startled you.' His dark eyes shuttled back to the patient before settling upon her again. His head didn't move once. 'Is he all right?'

'Confused,' she replied, 'but that's only to be expected. I examined him for any evidence of side-effects, but he appears to be all right apart from acute weakness. It might be a good idea if we take a blood sample and check it for any disorders.'

He inclined his regal head. 'I will see to it,' he replied gently. 'Very good, Nurse Crane. I'll leave you to your duties. I only stopped by to see how you were coping.'

'Yes, Doctor.'

'I'll relieve you at seven-thirty,' he continued as he turned back to the door. 'Then you may consider the rest of the evening as your own. Unless I need to call for you, that is.'

He paused with one hand on the knob. 'Oh, by the way — '

'Yes, Doctor?'

'I wonder if you might allow me to take you to dinner one of these evenings? There is a very good restaurant in York that I have grown particularly fond of. I think you would like it also.'

She was taken aback by his unexpected invitation, and it left her a little flustered. 'Uh, I'm sure I would, but well, what about our patient?' Again she refused to use the silly name Mr Ozerov had given him.

Dr Miros' brown eyes roved back to the young man in the bed. 'I'm sure he won't miss us,' he replied with a carelessness that secretly shocked her. 'He is in no real danger, anyway. Yasha Schulmann could keep an eye on him for a couple of hours, and she would know where to reach us if she had to.' His smile came back, wider than ever. 'Anyway, think about it and let me know.'

'Very good, Doctor. Thank you.'

He left the room soundlessly. Even the door closed silently behind him.

As soon as he was gone, Lynn sagged. Although she'd only known Dr Miros for a few hours, she had no intention of mixing business with pleasure, no matter how charming he might be. It was extremely unprofessional, for one thing, and for another — there was something about the good doctor that made her flesh creep.

She turned back to her patient, dismissing Miros from her mind as she recalled the last words the young man had spoken to her. Only two, barely audible words, yet she found them oddly disturbing.

Just before he'd lost consciousness, he had murmured, 'Help me.'

★   ★   ★

True to his word, Dr Miros relieved her at seven-thirty, and because she had no appetite, she made her way straight up to her rooms. It had been a long and eventful day, and she was tired. As soon as she reached her quarters, she would shower and then have an early night.

The first thing she saw when she let herself through the door was a suitcase and a flight bag. Hurrying across to the luggage, she unzipped the bag and quickly rummaged through it. A few changes of clothes, some old and much-loved books and mementos — just the sight of them alone was enough to lift her flagging spirits.

The following morning at breakfast in the large, cosy kitchen downstairs, Lynn met the rest of the household. They were all Russian men, big, scowling and largely uncommunicative. Once introductions had been made, she asked Yasha Schulmann if she might have her car and flat keys back.

The burly, flat-faced secretary gave her a blank look. 'Keys?' she echoed.

Patiently, Lynn explained that Mr Ozerov had taken them the day before. Now that some of her things had been brought from her flat, and her car had been parked at the back of the house, she would like them returned.

'I will look into it,' the secretary promised formally and there was no real reason to doubt her, but Lynn got the uncomfortable feeling that she was being stalled, that, while they kept her keys, she was as good as a prisoner here.

Again she was willing to dismiss the notion as just a figment of an increasingly over-active imagination, but she would definitely feel happier when she had the keys back in her possession.

Refusing the offer of a full breakfast, she made do with toast and tea, and then hurried upstairs to see how her patient was faring today.

According to Dr Miros, there was no real change, and none expected for the time being. As soon as she was alone, however, Lynn checked the young man's chart for herself. Although she hated to confess it, Dr Miros seemed far too indifferent to his patient's welfare for her liking.

Apparently the young man had spent a peaceful night, which was good. Next she took his temperature. It was normal. Frowning, she ran a palm over his sheets. They were warm and dry, which was unusual because malaria sufferers usually perspired so heavily whilst in the throes of the disease that they would literally drench their bed-clothes.

She heard a car coming up the drive and hurried over to the window. It was a big, heavy black sedan, polished to a high gleam. Evidently it was someone important, then. The car crackled across the gravel courtyard below and came to a halt. As the doors opened, Mr Ozerov came down the steps to meet the newcomers. Her patient began to stir just then, and she turned back to him before she could discover who the new arrivals were.

For Lynn, the morning passed in an agony of indecision. She had only been here for one day. It wasn't her place to question Dr Miros' professional judgement, and yet she knew she could not stand by and remain silent. So, when the doctor stopped in at midday to see how things were, she finally gave voice to what had been playing on her mind.

'I don't wish to speak out of turn,' she began, uncomfortably. 'But — '

'Yes?' he prompted, curiously.

She decided to take the plunge. 'This patient, Doctor. He's like no malaria patient I've ever seen before.'

'And you have seen quite a few, have you?' he asked.

'Well . . . enough to know that this man isn't exhibiting any of the signs I would normally associate with the disease.'

She watched him carefully, hoping he wouldn't explode. Much to her surprise, however, he took it quite calmly.

'You mean that just because he isn't shivering and shaking, or vomiting and raving, you don't think he has malaria.

Is that what you are saying, Nurse Crane? Perhaps you would prefer a second opinion?'

'Please, Doctor Miros, I don't mean to give offence. It's just that — '

'It's just that,' he interrupted, his tone softening, 'you are an extraordinarily conscientious nurse and you are concerned for the welfare of your patient.'

He put a hand on her shoulder and gave it a squeeze.

'And for that, you are to be commended. But I can assure you, I have treated Mr X here for malaria several times in the last few years. This particular strain can sometimes manifest itself in many different ways, remember. Added to which, there are the drugs I have prescribed.'

'Oh?'

'Yes. By trial and error, I have been able to balance all the chemicals to bring about the strongest possible remedy with the least possible side-effects, expressly for this patient. If he does not exhibit the symptoms you would normally associate with malaria, that would seem to indicate that I am actually doing a good job, yes?'

Feeling slightly foolish for over-reacting, Lynn cast her eyes downward.

'Yes, Doctor. I didn't mean to question your diagnosis.'

'I know you didn't. And I know you won't let it happen again, but I am pleased to see that you're not afraid to think for yourself, and challenge the findings of others.'

He gave her shoulder another, rather familiar squeeze, and she had to fight the urge to cringe beneath his touch. Then he turned and left her alone, and although she knew she should feel more settled now that she had raised the question and received an answer, she didn't. She felt more restless and troubled than ever, because she knew, without any question of doubt, that Dr Vitale Miros had been lying through his teeth.

It was an uncharitable thought, and she took no satisfaction from it. But if she was right, if he was lying — why? Was the true nature of her patient's illness being hidden for reasons of security again? Who was this young man? What was really wrong with him? Why did she feel so certain, now, that she was a prisoner here, and why had the young man been asking her to help him?

There were so many questions in her mind that she could hardly think straight, and had to make a supreme effort to calm down and get the situation back into perspective. There was probably a perfectly reasonable explanation for everything. Dr Miros might even have been telling the absolute truth just now. But . . .

Irritably, she shook her head and told herself that she was letting her imagination get the better of her. This isolated, old house could take some of the blame for that; that and the fact that she was the only English girl among a staff of mostly close-mouthed Russians. Yes, that was it.

She went into the outer office and sat at Dr Miros' desk so that she could update the patient's notes. Almost as soon as she settled into his chair, however, her eyes fell to the telephone sitting at an angle to the left of his blotter.

Of course! She didn't know why she hadn't thought of it before. All she needed was a link with the outside world. That was the real cause of all her problems. She was just feeling lonely.

Although she was reluctant to use the phone without permission, she didn't think a short call would hurt. Tentatively she picked up the receiver, felt an absurd sense of gratitude when she heard the dialling tone, and quickly keyed in the number of Natalie Blake, a friend in London with whom she had gone through nursing college.

As the connection went through, Lynn told herself that she had been behaving foolishly, and that even the briefest of chats with Natalie, her closest friend, would soon put her back on track.

She heard ringing at the other end of the line. On the third ring, the call was answered. Natalie's voice said, 'Hello?'

Lynn's relief washed through her in a weakening tide.

'Hello, Natalie? It's me, Ly — '

There was a click and the line went dead.

For a moment Lynn was too stunned to realise properly what had happened. Then she put the receiver down slowly.

Had she been cut off deliberately, or was it just an accident? On impulse, she picked up the receiver again and listened.

This time there was no dialling tone.

She put the phone down, turned in the chair and looked around the room. Her spirits fell swiftly and a sick feeling settled in the pit of her tummy.

No, please, don't let it really be true, she begged mentally. Don't tell me I really am a prisoner here.

⋆ ⋆ ⋆

When Lynn went back to her patient, she found him awake again, staring around the room through confused, grey eyes, trying to make all the fragmented memories of the past few days jigsaw into place. He was not immediately aware of Lynn's presence, but when she came to stand beside the bed and check his pulse, that urgent, frantic look sharpened his gaze once more, and he grabbed weakly for her hand and tried to speak.

She could make no sense from his incoherent gruntings, and went to fetch him a glass of water. He drank some down, then shook his head lifelessly to say that he'd had his fill. She lowered his head back to the pillow, plumped it up gently around him and then straightened his bedsheets. In that moment all of her own doubts and worries were once again set aside as she concentrated only on seeing to his comfort.

46

He looked up at her and said slowly, 'Lynn . . . '

She smiled down at him in mild surprise, pleased that he had remembered her name. 'That's right,' she said, automatically switching to Russian.

'Please . . . ' He gasped. 'Help . . . me . . . '

'We are helping you,' she replied. 'You've been ill, but we're looking after you now.'

He shook his head. 'No . . . I . . . they . . . ' But before he could say more, his voice trailed off and he fell into a wandering, semi-conscious state.

Lynn chewed on her lower lip, torn between a desire to leave all the real or imagined intrigues of this place behind her and a desire to stay and care for the young man in her charge.

Oh, stop all this, she snapped at herself angrily. Instead of worrying about yourself all the time, you should be concentrating on him.

She looked down at her patient, at his finely-chiselled face, the sketching of manly bristles tracing a path up into his thick, black hair. In any other circumstances he would have been a strikingly handsome man. Again she tidied the bedsheets around him, noting the broadness of his muscular shoulders, the gentle sensitivity of his fine, long-fingered hands.

Yes, she thought. I should be concentrating on you.

★ ★ ★

The remainder of the day passed without event until Dr Miros relieved her again at seven-thirty that evening. Lynn immediately went downstairs to the kitchen in search of Yasha Schulmann. The austere, blonde woman was just finishing her evening meal when Lynn walked in and took her place at the table. The elderly cook immediately fetched a steaming meal from the big, old range and set it before her.

Lynn nodded a thank you to the woman and picked up her knife and fork. Before she began to eat, however, she once again asked Yasha for her keys.

Again the secretary gave her a blank look. 'Keys?' she repeated.

'Yes. I asked you about them this morning. Remember?'

Memory showed on the secretary's face. 'Ah, yes.'

'Well, may I have them?'

'I am afraid not. I have not been able to get them from Mr Ozerov yet. He has been in conference all day.'

'Well, I'd appreciate it if I could have them back as soon as possible.'

'I will see to it.'

Lynn chewed for a while, then asked with elaborate casualness, 'Oh, by the way — I was wondering. Is there a telephone I could use anywhere in the house? I'd like to call one of my friends and let her know where she can reach me.'

Yasha's stony expression gave nothing away. 'My office is closed now,' she said, 'but if you wish to call in any time tomorrow, you may use my phone. Or I will pass any messages along on your behalf.'

'No, that's all right, thank you. I'll make my own calls.'

The secretary shrugged. 'As you wish.'

After eating, Lynn went for a walk in the grounds close to the house, then retired early and spent the evening flipping idly through magazines and watching the sun slant even lower until it was lost behind the trees to the west. Her restlessness refused to go away, so she decided that the best thing she could do was go to bed and hope that things would look better, or at least make more sense, tomorrow.

She undressed in the darkness, showered and then slipped between the cool, cotton sheets.

Sleep did not come immediately, but she hadn't expected that it would. She lay on her back, staring up at the shadowed ceiling, listening to the stillness of the surrounding country-side. Again her thoughts turned to her handsome patient, just two floors down from where she was now. In her mind she remembered the way his deep but weakened voice had spoken her name. It might be unethical in the extreme, but even the memory of it alone was enough to send a tingle across her skin.

Sleep eventually claimed her, and almost before she knew it, dreams and reality had woven themselves together to form a procession of senseless, disquieting images from which she eventually awoke with a start a few hours later.

She came up on to her elbows, breathing hard, perspiring faintly, the bedsheets rucked up around her. For a moment she stared into the darkness, still confused, but slowly her breathing returned to normal and she glanced over to her bedside clock. It was a little after one in the morning.

Throwing back the sheets, she sat up. Her last memory was of her patient, calling for her. She could still hear his voice clearly in her mind, crying out,

'Lynn! Lynn! LYNN!'

But had that been real or just the tail-end of another dream? She listened to the darkness, but heard no other sounds. She told herself that she had only been dreaming after all, but knew she wouldn't be able to go back to sleep until she had checked on him.

Getting up, she slipped on her dressing-gown and hastily pulled on her slippers. A moment later, she closed her door behind her softly and padded down the darkened hallway to the staircase.

Around her, the house was cloaked in silence and shadow. Suits of armour watched her descent through blind visors. Somewhere down on the ground floor she thought she heard a low babble of conversation and then a sudden, short-lived burst of laughter. She crept on down the stairs, every small creak of wood magnified by her heightened senses.

Just as she reached the first-floor gallery, a door downstairs opened and an oblong of light fell across the expensive rugs and ornate wooden tiling directly below. Suddenly the men's voices grew louder as they came out into the reception area.

Instinctively Lynn froze where she was, and listened. The men were speaking Russian, but speaking it so quickly, and more than one at a time, that she couldn't translate it.

On impulse she crept forward to the ornamental balustrade and peered over. Four men had gathered immediately below her, and were saying their farewells. The visitors who had arrived in the large, black car earlier? There was a very good chance.

Lynn recognised the severe crop of Mr Ozerov's blond-grey hair as he shook hands with all the men in turn. So, she thought, Yasha had been telling the truth about that, at least. He had been in conference.

She turned her attention to the visitors. They were all dressed in dark suits, plain ties, white shirts that stood out starkly in the low light. Two of them she didn't recognise, but the third looked faintly familiar.

Then she caught her breath in surprise, for as they turned towards the door, a stray bar of light fell upon the third man's smooth, handsome face.

He was the last person she had been expecting to see.

It was him — her patient, Mr X!

3

Unable to believe the speed of his apparent recovery, Lynn stumbled back, away from the balustrade, and quickly retraced her steps back to her quarters.

When she reached her room, she closed the door behind her and leaned against the panels, waiting for the mad beating of her heart to slow.

Outside, she heard the big, black car crackle across the gravel courtyard and then glide away down the slim lane.

Her mind was in turmoil. What did it all mean? Why had these people employed her to look after a perfectly healthy man?

But almost at once she checked herself. Although she doubted that her patient had been ill with malaria, as Dr Miros was claiming, he had definitely been ill with something, but what?

Confused and, yes, frightened now,

Lynn made a decision. She had no idea what was really going on here, and an innate sense of caution told her that she was probably better off not finding out. One thing was sure, however. She wanted no part in it. For some reason that was beyond her, she had been lied to, misled and fobbed off.

As soon as she could get her hands on her keys, she was leaving this sinister house without a backward glance.

Sleep proved to be elusive for the remainder of the night, and the best she was able to manage was a light, troubled doze. She woke early, showered, donned her uniform and went downstairs to breakfast. Although she had little appetite and wanted only to leave, she was still just curious enough to want to hear Dr Miros' excuse for his patient's sudden recovery and absence as well.

Again she reminded Yasha Schulmann about her keys, and forced the issue by saying she would collect them from Yasha's office at lunchtime.

The secretary's flinty eyes scanned her face. Did she suspect that Lynn was really planning to leave before they could stop her? She forced herself to meet Yasha's gaze unblinkingly.

Yasha nodded, finally, and when she spoke, her voice lost some of its natural harshness. 'Very good, Nurse Crane.'

Lynn forced herself to eat some toast. She wasn't sure why, but she thought it might be best to act as naturally as she could, so as not to alert her employers to the course of action she had elected to follow. After breakfast, she excused herself and went directly up to Dr Miros' office.

The tall, athletic doctor rose from his chair as she came through the door, and greeted her with a smile and a nod.

Seemingly casually, Lynn said, 'Good-morning, Doctor. How is our patient today?'

Miros shrugged. 'About the same.'

That was not the reply she had been expecting, and with sudden daring, she tried to push the matter.

'Did you take that blood sample after all, or did you want me to do it this morning?' she asked.

He frowned, clearly not remembering. 'Blood sample?'

'We agreed that it might be a good idea to check his blood for any disorders,' she reminded him.

'Oh, yes, that's right,' he replied, demonstrating once again his scandalous lack of interest and commitment. 'Yes, I took it. I — ah — plan to analyse it later today.'

Doctor, Lynn thought gravely, you're lying again, and we both know it. But, aloud, all she said was, 'I'll just go in and take a look at him.'

To her surprise, Miros raised no objection, merely took the key from his pocket and handed it over to her. She crossed to the door, unlocked it and went through.

Her patient was in the bed, stretched out on his back, breathing deeply, sweating gently.

More confused than ever now, she

went quickly to his bedside and inspected him thoroughly. Was she going mad? She knew she had seen him the night before, fully conscious and aware of his surroundings, standing, walking — even laughing as he and Mr Ozerov shared a parting handshake. But . . .

She reached down, tenderly thumbed one of his eyelids back. No, there could be no faking it. He was definitely unconscious, and obviously ill.

Then she looked even closer at him, and went cold.

The man she had seen last night had been clean-shaven — but the man in the bed this morning was still sporting the better part of a week's growth of bristles on his chin! Hastily she struggled to dredge last night's memory of him back to the surface. Yes . . . yes, there was no mistake. The light had been poor, admittedly, but she had seen him clearly enough to notice that he was clean-shaven.

Again, she asked herself what it all

meant and, again, she had no answers. Whoever he really was, the man in the bed before her now still needed her help. She could not abandon him, and that was exactly what she would be doing if she left this place as she had been planning. No, he still needed her help, and there was no question in her mind; she had to give it.

'I will see you later, Nurse Crane.'

Lynn turned around. She wished that Dr Miros wouldn't ghost up behind her that way, but she kept her face carefully neutral as she said, 'Yes, Doctor.'

He was holding a sheaf of papers under one arm.

'If, for any reason, you need me,' he said, 'you know where to reach me.'

'Yes, Doctor, I know,' Lynn confirmed, then, 'Doctor?'

'Hmm?'

Lynn had never dreamed she could act so well. Off-handedly, as if it had just occurred to her, she said, 'I wonder if I could take an hour off this afternoon. I need to go into York for one or two things.'

His lips thinned down. 'Is it really necessary?' he asked, a little testily.

Innocently she said, 'I'm afraid so. I don't want to put you to any inconvenience, of course, but it is rather important.'

Reluctantly he nodded, and with a sigh said, 'All right. I will stand in for you for an hour at lunchtime, but try not to be too long.'

'Thank you. You're very kind.'

He waved one hand in a gesture that was typical of him.

'Kindness has nothing to do with it,' he replied. 'I just want to put you in my debt so that you will have to take me up on my dinner invitation.'

Stalling him, she said, 'All right, then. Shall we say Friday evening?'

'Certainly. I shall look forward to it.'

He left her alone and she went over to the bedside cabinet, where she picked up the bottles containing her patient's medications. She scanned them thoroughly, but the handwritten labels gave little away. As discreetly as she could, just in case there were hidden cameras around, she slipped a couple of tablets into her uniform pocket. Then her eyes travelled to the clock on the wall, and she started willing the time to pass.

★   ★   ★

Miros returned at midday, and with some trepidation, Lynn went straight down to Yasha's office. When she arrived, the sturdy, thick-set secretary gave her an enquiring glance, and, suddenly nervous, dreading another excuse, Lynn had to struggle to speak around the lump in her throat.

'I've come for my keys,' she said in a small voice.

Yasha looked at her for a long moment, her heavily-powdered face betraying nothing. Then, just when it seemed inevitable that the secretary would try to stonewall her with yet another glib evasion, she said, 'Here they are,' and she held Lynn's key-ring aloft.

Lynn was so pleased to actually see the keys again that she had to caution herself against snatching them. She thanked the other woman and hurriedly left before Yasha could ask for them back.

Fighting the compulsion to run, Lynn left the house and walked briskly around to the garages at the rear. She found them with little problem, located her car and climbed inside. So great was her haste by this time, so flustered was she by the events of the last few days, that she had difficulty fitting the key into the ignition at first. Finally, she was able to start the car, and the familiar growl of its engine made her feel ridiculously, childishly happy.

She clicked her seat-belt into place and sat there for a moment, letting the engine warm up. She could drive away from here now and put the whole sorry business behind her, perhaps send for her things later. There was nothing stopping her — apart from her patient, of course.

He was relying on her to help him. And she would, too — if she could.

She put the car into gear and steered it carefully out of the garage. Within moments, she was leaving the fortified manor house behind her, zipping along the deserted country lane and heading for the city.

She had considered driving straight to the nearest police station and confiding her suspicions about what was going on back at the house, but she doubted that the police would take her seriously. No crime had been committed, so far as she could tell. And without hard evidence, the police were hardly likely to act. Surmise, a simple gut feeling — they weren't enough.

She was on her own in this, but not entirely alone.

For the first time in days she began to feel the tension leaving her. Then she glanced in her rear-view mirror and noticed that a pale-blue car was following her, at a distance of approximately fifty yards.

Lynn felt a sudden stab of dread that brought her back to earth with a bump, and she had to force herself to concentrate more on negotiating the winding country lane.

She drove on, still trying to calm her rising agitation. She didn't recognise the car. She hadn't seen it in the garage where her own had been parked. And there was no reason why it should have any connection with the house she had just left. She narrowed her eyes into the rear-view mirror and tried to make out any details of the driver, but all she could see was a silhouette.

The car stayed behind her all the way to York, but even that was no real proof that she was being followed. At last the city came into sight, with its narrow roads and slim ribbons of pavement, and its pleasing mixture of modern and mediaeval buildings, all of its presided over by the famous Minster.

Lynn drew comfort from the crowds

of people. Soon the pale-blue car was lost in a whole line of traffic, and she began to feel a bit better. She found a parking space and drew in. She slotted some coins into the meter, took one final guarded look up and down the picturesque street, then set off at a walk.

Still not totally convinced that she wasn't being followed, however, Lynn deliberately dodged into a department store and weaved a hurried path around all the counters and displays until she could leave again by a side entrance. She did this in a few stores, to lose any possible pursuers.

Finally she located a phone box in a fairly quiet part of town. She keyed in a number with one trembling finger. After a few moments, an impersonal voice said into her ear, 'Gordon Pharmaceuticals. May I help you?'

Lynn cleared her throat.

'Yes. Could I have extension four-two-two-three, please?'

'Connecting you now.'

There was more ringing. Then another voice said, 'Labs.'

'Could I speak to Andrew Palmer, please?'

'Sure. Who's calling?'

'Lynn Crane.'

Lynn waited anxiously, willing Andrew to come to the phone quickly. She glanced along the street, but as near as she could see, she was all alone. Andrew Palmer was another friend from her nursing college days. Ganglingly tall, bespectacled and with an unruly mop of red-fair hair that no barber seemed able to tame, Andrew had been studying pharmacology. Now he worked in the research and development department of a large pharmaceuticals company.

At last his voice came on to the line, as warm and welcoming as ever.

'Lynn?'

'Hello, Andrew. I'm not interrupting anything, am I?'

'Oh, just an experiment that might validate twenty-five years of painstaking research,' he replied airily. 'Nothing that can't wait. How are you?'

'I'm fine,' she lied. 'Listen — I need to ask you a favour.'

'Anything but money,' he joked.

'I need to have some tablets analysed. I want to know exactly what's in them.'

'No problem.'

'Well, there might be just one,' she said.

'Oh?'

'I'd like it done in confidence,' she told him. 'Just between you and me.'

There was a long pause. Then Andrew's voice said, 'Is everything all right? You're not in any trouble, are you?'

'No, but I really need to know what's in these tablets.'

'I suppose I could run a few tests,' he hazarded.

'Only if you're sure you won't get yourself into any bother.'

'Don't you worry about me, my girl. Whereabouts are you? Can you drop them in? It'd be great to see you again.'

'I'm working up in Yorkshire at the

moment, but if I put them in the post to you, first class, do you think you might have some information for me by the end of the week?'

'I could try. Send them straight to my home address.'

'I will, Andrew. Thanks.'

'Are you sure you're all right, Lynn? You sound a bit low.'

'I'm just a bit homesick, that's all.'

They chattered on for another minute or so, then Lynn broke the connection and went directly to the nearest post office, where she bought a small, padded envelope, slipped the tablets she'd taken earlier into it, sealed it, stamped it and then posted it. She felt better for having set wheels in motion, and finally done something to help her make sense out of the events surrounding her stay at the old manor house.

She made her way back to the car, let herself inside and sat there for a moment or two. The day was bright and warm. Around her, people were going about their everyday business, seemingly without a care in the world. Lynn longed to be a part of it, and, once again, she told herself that it would be so easy just to keep driving south.

But she had a commitment of sorts here, and he was waiting for her to return. With reluctance she turned the car around and drove back to the manor.

★   ★   ★

Twenty minutes later, Lynn drove past the stony-faced security men at the gatehouse, parked the car where she had found it and went into the manor with dread settling heavily on her tummy.

In the reception area, she bumped into Mr Ozerov, who was just coming down the stairs.

The smiling administrator regarded her through his thick, polished lenses for a long moment before he finally spoke.

'Ah, Nurse Crane,' he said, 'back so soon? Dr Miros was telling me you had some business to attend to in York.'

'Not business,' she replied as calmly as she could. 'Only some shopping.'

He inspected her as he nodded his understanding.

'And did you get what you wanted?'

She realised then that she wasn't carrying anything to substantiate her story, and shook her head. 'No, I'm afraid I was out of luck.'

'Never mind,' he said. 'Perhaps next time.'

'Yes.'

She hurried past him and ascended the staircase to the first floor. Within moments she had reached the make-shift surgery.

When Dr Miros was gone, Lynn sank into his chair. She was exhausted by tension, and not completely sure that her employers had been taken in by her fictitious shopping trip. Still, at least she had made contact with Andrew Palmer, that was something.

Regaining her breath, Lynn unlocked the connecting door and went through to check on her patient. He was stirring weakly beneath his sheets, and moaning softly as he struggled mightily with inner demons.

Lynn heard a car crunching across the gravel drive below, and went over to the barred window. A small, horrified sound escaped from her throat when she saw the same pale-blue car that had followed her into York now turning around towards the back of the building.

So she *had* been followed! The confirmation had a stunning effect upon her, and made her head swim. Quickly she told herself that her employers were probably keeping an eye on her as a matter of routine. It didn't necessarily mean that they suspected her of anything . . .

She thought back to her visit to York. Had she successfully eluded them in the sprawling city? She thought so, but would they suspect that she had done so deliberately, or be content that they themselves had simply lost sight of her?

'Uhhh . . .'

She turned away from the window and gasped again. Her patient had regained consciousness and somehow managed to climb out of bed. He looked at her now, naked from the waist up, his broad torso glistening, his powerful arms reaching towards her, his lips opening and closing as he tried to form a plea of sorts.

Lynn hurried to him just as he slumped forward and stumbled into her arms. For a moment then they were locked into an awkward embrace, her arms around his body, his arms encircling her shoulders, his head lolling next to her, his face within inches of her own . . .

He looked right at her, his grey eyes burning deep into her blue ones. She felt the warmth radiating out of him, seeping through her uniform to warm her own chilled skin. She was close enough to see every individual hair on

73

his chin, close enough to smell the strong, male scent of him . . .

Then she felt the life go out of him and quickly got him on to the bed before his legs buckled altogether.

She put her hands on his chest and eased him down on to his back, then bent, raised his legs and gently twisted him around so that he was laying flat along the mattress again. He had accidentally disconnected the drip in his right arm, and she quickly moved to replace it. As she did so, however, he opened his eyes again and whispered her name.

At once she gave his hand a squeeze. 'I'm here,' she said. 'Just relax.'

He shook his head, swallowed a few times. Clearly he had no intention of relaxing, at least not yet. 'You . . . you're not . . . Russian?' he croaked.

'No.'

'B-but . . . you speak my . . . language?'

'Yes. A little.'

'Then . . . you m-must . . . help me.'

'I am helping you,' she said.

Again he shook his head, his face twisting into a mask of irritation and despair.

'I'm . . . not sick,' he said huskily.

Lowering her own voice, Lynn said, 'I know.'

He stared at her, realising exactly what she was trying to say to him, but she was afraid to confide any more in case he unwittingly repeated it to Dr Miros. For the time being, the least said was best.

Still, he seemed to take comfort from even the little she had said, and unable to fight against it any longer, closed his eyes and fell back into a deep slumber.

Lynn ran her eyes over him, feeling more determined than ever to help him.

She checked the time and then glanced at the tablets on the bedside cabinet. For a long time she debated the course of action she intended to take. At last she reached her decision. Sensing that his medication was at least partly to blame for his condition, she would give her nameless patient no more of it until she learned from Andrew exactly what was in it. Even if Dr Miros continued to administer it, her patient would only now receive half his current dose.

The next two days passed without event. At her suggestion, Dr Miros and Lynn changed shifts so that she would tend to their patient through the darkness hours and he could care for him by day. Although it went against her training to deliberately withhold her patient's treatment, she continued to do so, and was certain that he began to respond. Certainly his periods of lucidity grew more prolonged, and it did her good to see the improvement in him.

On Friday morning, Dr Miros reminded her about their dinner engagement for that evening. As if she could forget! Although she had been dreading it, she was determined to use it to her advantage. Thus, with Yasha keeping an eye on their patient, they drove to York in the doctor's car, and dined at a softly-lit, intimate restaurant.

The food was marvellous, but Lynn was so preoccupied and nervous that the taste of it hardly registered with her.

For his part, Dr Miros was the perfect host, and ensured that the conversation never flagged. He spoke eloquently of his beloved country, of its people and the beauty of its fine beaches at sunset, with the waters of the Baltic lapping at its golden sands. He was a charming companion, of that there could be no doubt, but he was a bit too charming for his own good, and Lynn remained wary of him.

Between the main course and dessert, Lynn excused herself from the candlelit table. Dr Miros rose from his chair, inclined his head and watched her leave the room.

Outside, she made straight for the pay-phone she'd noticed on the way in. She glanced self-consciously over her shoulder, convinced herself that she wasn't being overlooked, then dialled

Andrew Palmer's home number.

He answered almost at once. 'Hello?'

'Hello, Andrew. It's me, Lynn.'

'Lynn! About those tablets — '

'You've run some tests on them, then?' she asked eagerly.

'Yes. They arrived yesterday morning. Listen, this is all very mysterious — '

'I'll explain it all in good time, Andrew, I promise. But, for now, what did you find out?'

'They're sedatives,' he replied directly. 'But they must have been manufactured privately, because there's nothing quite so strong on the open market, at least not to my knowledge.'

'What do you mean, strong?' she prompted uneasily.

'Well,' Andrew said, 'basically they're a compound of three different drugs. It's a pretty lethal cocktail, let me tell you. Even a bull elephant would have a hard time fighting against that little lot.'

'You didn't find any quinine, then?' Lynn asked. 'Any malaria treatments at all?'

'No. I told you, the tablets you sent me are sedatives,' Andrew replied firmly. 'Listen, Lynn, I don't know what this is all about, but I think you should know this much. If you keep administering these tablets for any length of time, one of these days your patient's just not going to wake up again.'

4

Stunned, Lynn replaced the receiver before she realised what she was doing and stood in the foyer for a few moments, trying to understand where this new fragment of the puzzle fitted in.

Try as she might, she still couldn't get any of it to make sense, and found her own helplessness frustrating.

Again she considered going to the police. All it would take was a phone call, and she would probably never get a better opportunity than now but, again, she decided against it. What could she tell them? She didn't know herself, yet.

No — she needed more information before she could successfully seek help from the authorities.

Realising that she had already been gone for some time, she composed herself as best she could and returned to her table. Dr Miros was as considerate as ever throughout the remainder of the evening, and she was somehow able to continue with the masquerade as if nothing was wrong, but, inside, she was a maelstrom of emotions, primary among them fear.

Eventually the evening came to an end and they drove back through the dark, hedge-enclosed lanes until the old manor loomed large before them.

Dr Miros parked his car behind the house and escorted her inside. It was quite late by then, and the house was dark and silent, but for the few lights that still burned on the ground floor.

At the foot of the staircase, Miros paused and gestured towards the sitting-room, which looked out on to the shadowed courtyard, and asked, 'Would you care for a nightcap, Lynn?'

Lynn just wanted to be left alone, but she masked her true feelings well enough.

'I'd better not, Doctor,' she said, quietly. 'But thank you for asking all the same. I ought to keep a clear head. I still have a night duty to get through.'

He nodded in understanding. 'Yes, perhaps you are right. I've an early start myself in the morning, haven't I?'

Her interest sharpened immediately. 'Have you?'

He squinted at her. 'Didn't Max tell you? We have to go to London for a few days, he and I, on business. I'm afraid you will have to look after Mr X all on your own.'

She found the news both surprising and, secretly, pleasing, though she disguised the latter emotion as well.

'I'll manage,' she said, to allay any suspicions he or Mr Ozerov might have about her.

'I'm sure you will,' he replied, putting a hand on her arm again in that familiar way she found so unpleasant. 'I'll be phoning in every so often anyway, just to make sure that everything is all right.'

'Well, if you'll excuse me, Dr Miros . . . '

'Oh, please,' came the urbane and gently insistent reply, 'call me Vitale.'

She was already backing up the staircase by then, nodding again just to keep him happy. 'Vitale.'

A few moments later she was back in her room, changing out of her flatteringly-cut, black dress and slipping into her altogether more sensible uniform. Her mind raced as she began to slot this latest piece of information into place and decide how best it might help her.

When she relieved Yasha Schulmann in the surgery a few minutes later, she was once again the personification of reason and control, proving, if only to herself, that these people weren't the only ones who could practise a little deception. Even as she watched Yasha leave the room, she marvelled at how well she was holding up — at least on the outside.

Left alone with her patient once more, Lynn checked his room as thoroughly as she could for any hidden cameras or listening devices. She didn't know exactly what she was expecting to find, of course, anything that looked out-of-place or suspicious, she supposed, but she found nothing.

Next she took a cool flannel and wiped her patient's rugged face, and when his glazed eyes flickered open she threw caution to the wind and went all out to revive him.

'What . . . ? I . . . '

'Come on, now,' she muttered determinedly in Russian. 'Shake yourself out of it now. That's the way. Come on, you can do it . . . '

It took time, far longer than she would have thought, because even at half the original dosage, his tablets had still been deadly strong.

'Come on, now. That's the way. Wake up now. You must wake up . . . '

An hour later, well into the total darkness of the country night, her patient was sitting up in bed, drinking glass after glass of water to flush out his system, and his deep, grey eyes were gradually clearing . . .

At last she said in an undertone, still fearful of being caught, 'How do you feel now?'

He looked at her for a long time, his eyes travelling over her face. By way of answer, he threw back his sheets and swung his legs over the edge of the bed. When he spoke, his voice was still husky, but strengthening all the while.

'I've got . . . to get out . . . of here.'

Immediately Lynn moved to restrain him, placing her palms on his bare, broad shoulders to keep him where he was.

'Now wait a minute,' she said, speaking urgently to make sure he understood the seriousness of their position. 'You're in no fit state to go anywhere, yet.'

'I'm not . . . sick,' he said, almost truculently.

'I know you're not. You've been drugged.'

His eyes, which he was keeping focused with a mighty effort, roved across her face with new interest. 'How did you know that? Who are you, anyway? Where do you fit into all this?'

'All what?' she countered. 'I only started working here a few days ago.'

His puzzlement showed in a frown. 'But — '

Quickly, Lynn told him how she came to be there, what she had been told about his illness and why she had taken the chance of cutting down his so-called medication and now reviving him more or less completely. He showed particular interest when she told him about the man she had seen a few nights before who resembled him so much.

In a way, it was a relief to unburden herself, to finally explain it all to someone who was only too willing to listen. But Lynn's side of the story was pitifully slim. There was still so much she didn't know.

'I don't even know your name,' she finished tiredly. 'I don't even know who you are.'

'And yet — ' He was still confused, struggling to put everything together and perhaps explain it all as much for his own benefit as hers. 'And yet,' he said again, 'you have done all this for me?'

She nodded mutely.

He glanced down at her hands, reached for one, held it. Running his tongue over his dry lips, he said, 'My poor girl, you're shaking. And you have every right to be afraid. I fear that you have become involved in a very dangerous game.'

That was really the last thing she wanted to hear, and she said again, 'Who are you?'

He sat up straighter, raised his head proudly, and said in his weak voice, 'I am Duke Serge Varda.'

Lynn shook her head again. A duke? No — it was all too much for her. She just couldn't take it in.

But she had to. This was her chance to finally get some answers. Her voice a whisper, she said, 'You're — you're royalty?'

She'd told herself as much that first

day, of course, when Dr Miros had made mention of a state visit, but she hadn't really believed it.

He nodded slowly, still trying to fully shake off the effects of the sedatives.

'Yes, I am royalty. And in a way, that is the key to this entire business.'

'I don't understand.' Her eyes questioned him. 'Why are you here?'

He gestured that she should sit beside him on the bed while he brought order to his thoughts.

'My country is small. It does not figure largely on the world stage. Until recently, we were a part of the USSR, but we are a proud people and we fought long and hard to achieve our independence. When it finally came, however, it brought with it great financial problems, not the least of which was our ailing economy.'

He fell silent for a time, as another wave of weakness washed over him. Then, steeling himself against it, he went on, gasping for breath as he forced out his words.

'For two years now I have worked behind the scenes to — to secure aid for my people. Your country has been kind and generous, but we do not want to live on charity. We want to work and earn, to make our own way in the world.

'Here, again, your country has been good to us, and, after much negotiation, we have formulated a trade agreement with you which I had come here to sign. At last, the long struggle of my people is nearly over. But — '

Lynn studied his profile, noting the passion that flared in his eyes and the sudden grimace that curled his lips as he shook his head.

'What?' she prompted in a hushed tone.

Swallowing hard, he continued. 'But power corrupts, and even the promise of power is enough to corrupt. Now that we seem poised to enjoy a better and more prosperous future, there are those who would — who would remove me from power in order to — to seize control of my country for themselves.'

'Mr Ozerov?' Lynn hazarded. 'Dr Miros?'

He nodded sadly. 'Yes. Once they were my trusted advisers, but now they are ruled by greed. I learned that too late. When we arrived here in your country they drugged me and imprisoned me here.'

Lynn said, 'I'm sorry, but I still don't really understand.'

He looked right into her face, his expression bleak.

'What is the date?' he asked suddenly.

She had been so preoccupied of late that she had to think before replying.

'It's the eighth. Friday the eighth.'

'I am due to sign the trade agreement at our embassy in London, on Tuesday. Your media will be there to — to witness it because they know how important it is for my country. If, for any reason, I fail to sign it, or I am seen to reject it out of hand, which is where this double of mine you saw comes in, well, another betrayal, even more hardship . . . ' He shook his head, the uselessness of his situation overwhelming him, suddenly. 'It would be more than my people could stand.

'A wave of rebellion, the likes of which you cannot even imagine, would sweep through the country. Overnight, there would be anarchy. Ozerov and Miros would take control — and under their régime, the agreement would be signed, but only they would ever see the benefits of it. Under their rule, my people would be as oppressed as ever.'

'That must be where Ozerov and Miros are going tomorrow,' Lynn said suddenly. 'To your embassy in London.'

He agreed. 'Yes, they — they would. They will need to school this double of mine — train him for the part he must play.'

Speaking without really being aware of it, Lynn said, 'But they'll never get away with it, surely? They can't keep you a prisoner here for ever, and this double they've found, he can't pretend to be you indefinitely. Sooner or later you must get your chance to denounce them.'

His eyes filled with a bitter sadness. 'In a sometimes evil world, your naïveté does you credit, Lynn,' he muttered.

'What do you mean, naïveté?'

'Ozerov and Miros are clever and ruthless men. They know they cannot continue with this pretence for ever. As long as I live, I am a danger to them. So, when the time is right, probably at the height of the expected backlash, they will arrange for a 'patriot' to 'assassinate' me, and that will tidy up all the loose ends for them, once and for all.'

He let his breath out slowly and said with a calm acceptance she found chilling, 'That is why they have kept me alive. So that they can produce a body when the time comes.'

Lynn went cold, and horror squeezed at her throat so that she found it hard to breathe.

'They're going to murder you?' Then

something else occurred to her. 'What about me? I'm a witness! I can confirm everything you've told me. Together we could — '

He shook his head and she fell silent. 'There will be no witnesses, Lynn. Do you understand what I am saying?'

Understanding struck her like a hammer-blow. 'You mean they plan to — to kill me, too?'

He nodded his head slowly.

Suddenly she felt herself thrown into total, blind panic, and tears stung her eyes. All at once she understood why Mr Ozerov had been so keen to employ a nurse who had few friends or relatives who would miss her.

'No,' she whispered a little desperately. 'No, you're wrong. You must be wrong.'

He reached up and held her by the shoulders, and his touch was gentle and comforting, his inner strength feeding through to her at exactly the moment she needed it.

'I am terribly sorry for you, Lynn.

You are just an innocent bystander in all this. You deserve better.' He nodded decisively. 'And I shall give you better. I swear it.'

He stood up, wavered slightly, and within moments she was there beside him, supporting him.

'You're still weak, um — I'm not sure how to address you,' she admitted shyly.

He looked at her and a grim smile quirked his mouth and completely altered the set of his face. 'You do not need to stand on ceremony with me, Lynn, you, of all people. To you I am, and always will be, just Serge.'

She nodded. 'All right, but I mean it. You're weak. You need time to recover.' An idea suggested itself to her. When she spoke it, her voice was trembling but purposeful. 'Look, now that I know what this is all about, I can drive you into York and fetch the police. I daren't use one of the phones here, otherwise I'd call them right away.'

'I doubt that you would get that far,'

Serge commented. 'Unless I am mistaken, Ozerov has posted guards here.'

'Yes.'

'Then you are as much a prisoner as I.'

'But I managed to slip into town the other day,' Lynn protested.

'Yes, but that was the other day. If anything, he will have increased security now that the moment of the signing is so near.'

Lynn felt her spirits sinking. 'What can we do, then? We must do something! We can't just let them . . . '

He raised one hand and put a finger to her lips to silence her. She could see that his reserves of energy were rapidly deserting him again, though he was fighting to remain conscious.

'We will do something,' he whispered. 'Somehow, I will get you away from this place, and, once you are safe from harm, I will — '

'You'll go to the police?' she asked.

He shook his head. 'I daren't. I couldn't be sure whom I could trust.

For all my country's poverty, Ozerov is still a powerful man. I cannot tell how far his influence has already spread.'

Resolve firmed his chin as he continued, breathing deeply with every phrase.

'No, I must denounce these traitors myself. Expose them for the deceivers they are — at exactly the moment they intend to reject the agreement. I must unmask them right there, at the embassy, before the assembled media and Press — '

At last Serge could fight against it no longer, and Lynn had to help him to sit on the edge of the mattress again.

'Serge — what you're suggesting is madness. How will you get away from here in your condition? Once Ozerov's men discover that we've gone, they'll come after us, hunt us down. We won't even get close to your embassy.'

'Then I'll just have to outwit them, slip away from here tomorrow night, then use any means of — of transport I can to — to reach London — even if I have to crawl there on my hands and knees.' His eyes rose to meet hers. 'But I will do it, Lynn — I must!'

'You'll need clothes, some food, money.' She looked at him and asked, 'How good is your English?'

Again that quirk of a smile ghosted his lips. 'Nowhere near as good as your Russian.'

'Then you'll need an interpreter as well.'

'You?' He shook his head. 'Oh, no. You're already in enough peril. I won't put you in any more danger. I just won't allow it.'

Impulsively now, inspired by his courage and determination, knowing that they were on their own in this, that they had no choice but to do as he had said, she talked him down.

'You're too late, Serge. I'm as much a target away from you as with you. At least if we're together, we have a greater chance of evading these men. If their plan is to do me harm, then I'm as determined as you are to bring them to justice.'

He looked at her, wonder coming into his eyes.

'You really mean that, don't you?' he murmured.

Steadfastly she brushed her earlier tears aside. 'Yes, I do.'

'Then — then we'll do it — the two of us. It will be a hard and difficult few days, but we will succeed. We must . . .'

She sensed that he was fading fast, and gently forced him to lay down again.

'Get some rest now, Serge. Leave everything to me.'

Within moments he was in a deep sleep, and Lynn was wondering apprehensively just what she had let herself in for.

★   ★   ★

There was so much to do that Lynn hardly knew where to begin, but at least she had the whole of Saturday to get herself organised, and by then she was feeling so jittery that it was good to have something to keep her occupied.

While Serge struggled to fight off the lingering after-effects of his medication, Lynn watched Ozerov and Miros climb into a big, black car and leave for London.

Feeling a little easier in her mind once they were gone, she set to work with pen and paper, and listed everything she had to do.

As soon as their absence was discovered, the plotters would be informed by telephone and would no doubt order a full-scale search at once. With a coolness she had never imagined she might possess, Lynn decided that they must slip away from the manor as early as they dare after dark, and travel all night to put as much distance as they could between themselves and their pursuers.

They could not risk taking her car. They must leave quietly and without fuss, so that meant going on foot, and, to further confound the opposition, they would have to take the least obvious route to their eventual destination.

Lynn felt doubts and misgivings creeping into her mind as she worked. A little voice kept undermining her confidence, telling her that her situation was hopeless, that her plan would never work, but she blotted it out doggedly. It must work. It had to.

They would need money. Lynn had some with her, and her credit card would enable her to get more direct from her savings account, as and when they needed it.

She thought about Serge. He was still too weak to undertake such a dangerous journey, but she sensed that the strength and depth of his convictions would see him through. Still, he would need clothes, and food to help him regain his former vitality.

The day passed without hurry. As early evening began to darken the sky at last, Lynn felt the strain beginning to take its toll on her. Perhaps it was just her imagination, but she felt sure that

Yasha Schulmann was keeping an even closer eye on her than usual, in the absence of her employer. She was careful to give nothing away, but, even so, Yasha had a disquieting influence on her.

At six o'clock, Lynn picked up the phone on Dr Miros' desk and asked to have her evening meal sent up to her. It was not an unusual request, given that she was there to monitor her patient, and when the meal was delivered, she took it straight through to Serge, who was now as restless to leave as she was.

'Here,' she said. 'Eat this while it's hot.'

He frowned at her. 'What about you?'

She gave a brief, humourless laugh and said, 'I've got no appetite.'

He looked at her very seriously. 'I wish you were not involved in this.'

'So do I,' she replied, honestly, 'but now that I am, I'm going to see it through to the end.'

He shook his head gently. 'You know,' he said, 'the women are strong in my country. Over the years, they've had to be, but I don't believe I've ever met a woman stronger than you.'

Lynn felt heat coming to her face at the compliment, a different kind of warmth building in her tummy at his nearness. To change the subject, she pointed to the plate she had fetched in.

'Eat it before it gets cold.'

He looked at the food. 'It's been so long since I've eaten solids, I've almost forgotten how to.'

'It'll soon come back to you,' she predicted, trying to match his attempt to lighten their spirits.

He watched her cross to the door and a frown suddenly ploughed into his forehead. 'Where are you going?'

Mysteriously she replied, 'Shopping.'

Half and hour later she was back, breathing heavily with suppressed tension and carrying a small bundle of clothes furtively under one arm.

'Here,' she said, putting them on the bed beside the duke. 'I've, uh . . . 'borrowed' these from Dr Miros' room. I think you and he should be about the same size.'

Serge stood up, astonishment registering on his handsome face as he separated out a freshly-laundered shirt, a sweater, a pair of dark trousers, underwear, a casual jacket — even a pair of sturdy, walking shoes. He gave a grim chuckle as his grey eyes came up to her face.

'You are full of surprises,' he muttered.

'That's not all,' Lynn said, reaching into a pocket of her uniform. 'Here.' And she handed him a small canister of shaving foam and a disposable razor, which she had appropriated from Dr Miros' en suite bathroom.

'Well, you have to look your best when you meet the Press on Tuesday,' she said, embarrassed. 'I'll pack them and take them with us.'

Ignoring the items she had set down on the bed, he came to stand before her and concentrate the full force of his personality on her.

'I will never be out of your debt, will I?' he asked quietly.

With high colour staining her cheeks, Lynn shrugged and tried to make light of it. 'Don't be silly. You don't owe me a thing.'

He towered over her, holding her eyes with his own, and again she was all too aware of his nearness, the heat pulsing out through the skin of his bare chest.

'I owe you for everything,' he insisted gently. 'My life. The chance to stop these traitors before they can succeed with their vile plan. You have given me all of this, and at great sacrifice to yourself.'

He reached out, took hold of her arms, and looked down into her face.

'I will repay you, Lynn. I promise. When this is all over, I will repay you a thousand times over, if I can.'

While the night grew even darker beyond the barred window, Lynn looked up at him and tried to understand the strange emotions warring inside her. Here she was, her life in danger, and yet as scared and nervous as she undoubtedly was, she seemed to forget how to be afraid when she was with Serge.

Although this was really neither the time nor the place, she had to admit she was attracted to him. If she was honest with herself, she had felt an attraction for him right from the first, a depth of feeling that went beyond compassion. But where was the future in that?

And yet, as she looked up into his shadowed eyes, she asked herself if it could be that he was beginning to feel for her what she knew she felt for him.

No, it couldn't be. He was simply grateful for the little she had done for him, that was all.

'How — how do you feel?' she asked, breaking the moment.

He nodded. 'All right. Still a little weak, but — ' He smiled. 'I'll make it.'

She swallowed audibly, her throat closing down as tension once again started building within her.

'You'd better get dressed now, while I

go to my room and collect a few bits and pieces.'

She looked around at their sparse, harshly-lit surroundings and couldn't wait to leave them for good, for the two of them to leave for good.

'We'll wait until midnight,' she said. 'And then we'll make our break for it.'

5

Midnight . . . Lynn thought it would never come. More than once she checked her watch, thinking that it might have stopped, but, no — time was just dragging, the way it always did when you wanted it to do just the opposite.

She had changed into a thick sweatshirt, a pair of jeans and trainers, and a dark anorak. Her money, credit card, everything she was likely to need, were all safely packed into her small shoulder bag. Now, as the hands of every watch and clock in the old, isolated manor edged closer to the witching hour, she exchanged a look with the man she was risking everything to help, and when his encouraging smile touched her, she felt the tension of the moment ebbing just a little.

At last, when she felt unable to wait

any longer, she said, 'Let's go.'

The surgery, like the rest of the house, was in darkness. Serge, now clean-shaven, opened the door as softly as he could, listened to the hissing silence, then peered outside. Cautiously he padded out into the hallway with Lynn at his heels. She closed the door softly behind her and looked up into Serge's night-greyed face. 'I'll lead the way,' she whispered.

She knew that, because of his chivalrous upbringing, he would have preferred to go ahead. They had discussed it at some length earlier on, but Lynn knew the layout of the big house — Serge didn't. So now she stole past all the empty suits of armour with Serge lagging reluctantly behind, until they reached the head of the stairs.

Here, a sudden gust of laughter drifting up from the staff quarters below stairs stopped them in their tracks. As the laughter subsided to a dull babble of conversation, they exchanged another loaded glance. All at once, the need for speed and silence was even more acute, if they were to leave without raising the alarm.

Serge's hand slipped warm and comforting around hers. As quietly as they could, they descended the broad staircase, Lynn hardly daring to take her eyes off the darkened doorway that led to the staff quarters.

They were halfway down the stairs when the huge grandfather clock beside the front door began to chime the hour. In the stillness of the night, it might as well have been Big Ben for all the noise it made.

Taken by surprise, Lynn and Serge broke stride, hesitated a moment, not sure whether to go back, stand their ground or descend the rest of the stairs and race straight for the front door.

On impulse, Lynn pressed on, and Serge followed. Through the darkness, the wide, front door came nearer. Lynn reached for the handle, almost forgetting to breathe in her haste, wishing that the grandfather clock would cease its insistent chiming so that she could concentrate more on what she was doing.

Through the door that led to the staff quarters they heard another peal of laughter. It reminded Lynn just how exposed they were now. If anyone should come through that door, she and Serge would be spotted at once.

Then the chiming stopped and near-silence settled back over the house. Breathing fast now, heart hammering, Lynn put her hand on the doorknob and was just about to turn it when she heard footsteps crunching over the gravel outside and realised with a sudden jolt that someone was approaching from the other side of the door!

She felt Serge stiffen beside her. He had heard it, too. She sagged a little, told herself that the worst had happened, that they were going to be discovered any moment now —

In despair, Lynn and Serge glanced around. Almost simultaneously their

110

eyes rested on the sitting-room to their left. Taking Serge by the hand again, drawing fresh strength from the firmness of his palm against hers, Lynn hurried them in that direction.

No sooner had they slipped into the sitting-room and pushed the door to a crack behind them than the front door swung open and the two big men Lynn had seen at the gatehouse a few times clattered inside, speaking loudly.

Serge put his eye to the gap and watched as one of the newcomers turned around and pushed home two big bolts to secure the door from the inside. Then the men stamped out of sight, and a moment later Lynn and Serge heard them heading for the staff quarters.

Lynn closed her eyes as an unexpected wave of weakness overtook her. Resolutely, she willed her heart to slow its crazy pounding.

She realised suddenly that she and Serge were holding each other close, that they had fallen into an embrace naturally and without forethought, and that it was a good and comforting place for her to be.

But they couldn't stay here for ever. They had to get away, and quickly.

They broke apart, each as seemingly reluctant to do so as the other, and Serge gestured to the french windows on the other side of the room. Lynn nodded and they crept quietly across to them.

Carefully, Serge unlocked them, opened one, went outside. Lynn watched him as he scanned the darkness. Finally he indicated that she should join him. Taking the key, she closed the door softly behind her and locked it.

She popped the key into her pocket, hoping that it wouldn't be missed, or that if it was, whoever needed it would assume that it had been mislaid, not stolen.

The night was cold and silent. The sky was a splash of purple velvet across which clouds scudded like puffs of cotton wool, and stars sparkled like diamonds. Lynn shivered. Serge felt the tremor run through her and put one arm protectively around her shoulders.

'Are you all right?' he whispered, vapour coming from between his lips with the question.

'Yes,' she replied.

They had come out at the side of the big manor, which put them on the blind side of the gatehouse at the front. On the far side of the courtyard, a row of bushes and dwarf pines punctured the skyline. Drawing in a deep breath, they crouch-ran towards the foliage, vanished into it, then waited, not breathing, just listening, half-expecting someone to raise the alarm at last.

Nothing happened.

They scanned the broad, sloping field that now stretched ahead, the dark, bulky silhouettes of hedgerows, elm trees.

'Which way?' Serge whispered.

Lynn pointed south, in the general direction of York, and sticking to cover as much as they could, they set off at a determined pace, leaving the house behind them.

★   ★   ★

The night was dreary and quiet but for the rustlings of small nocturnal animals. After a while they came out on to the York road and plodded doggedly on. A light drizzle seeped through to the bone and made the winding lane ahead glisten blackly.

After about two hours, they sheltered beneath a huge elm, to catch their breath and wait out the heaviest shower so far. Serge was breathing rapidly, and his face was damp with sweat as he leaned against the gnarled trunk.

Examining him worriedly in the poor light, Lynn said, 'Are you all right?'

He nodded uncertainly. 'Yes — yes — it's just . . . '

She reached for his wrist and took his pulse. It was racing.

'You're still weak,' she said. 'Those

tablets took more out of you than we realised.'

He glanced down at her. 'You're probably right,' he agreed. 'But don't worry. I'll get over it.'

A short time later they started off again. Lynn was too keyed-up to feel tired, but she could sense the glassiness of her eyes as they marched on down the night-enshrouded lane. She wondered how long they had before someone back at the house noticed that they were gone and the chase really began. She had a nasty feeling that their head start would vanish all too quickly when that time came.

About ninety minutes later, the spires and roofs of York came into sight, and they found their flagging spirits lifting. Lynn checked the time. It was a little before four o'clock in the morning, too early for the buses and trains to be running, even if they could have risked catching one. On the outskirts of the city, they found a petrol station that was open all night, and going inside, Lynn bought a local map, two soft drinks and some chocolate, which would keep their energy up until they could buy something more substantial.

Outside again, they found a sheltered spot close to the city's north wall and rested while Lynn pored over the map by the bright light of a streetlamp.

'Where do we go from here?' Serge asked wearily.

At length she said, 'We need to get on to the A19 for Selby.'

Wearily, they got up and walked through the slowly-waking city, past the River Ouse until they came to the Fulford Road. It started to rain again, pattering persistently against the leaves in nearby Rowntree Park and stippling the surface of the river with a million pinpricks.

★   ★   ★

At about five-thirty, yellow headlights suddenly swept up behind them and a car horn bleated twice. Lynn, who by then was concentrating solely on just putting one foot in front of the other, suddenly wheeled around, fearing the worst — then relaxed slightly when she saw a man with a ruddy, cheerful face leaning out of the cab of a big blue lorry.

'You've picked a right time to go hiking, haven't you?' he called down, his battered face lit by the red and green lights on his dashboard. 'Where're you going?'

Lynn called up, 'London.'

'I can drop you at Doncaster, if that's any good,' the lorry driver offered.

Lynn nodded eagerly. 'That would be marvellous. Thank you.' And Serge echoed her in halting English. 'Yes, thank you.'

'Hop in, then.'

Quickly Lynn and Serge climbed into the cab. The driver eased the lorry back into the light flow of early-morning traffic and the lights of York began to recede.

There was plenty of room to stretch

out and rest their aching legs. The driver seemed content to listen to his radio, so Lynn and Serge closed their eyes. Relaxed by the gentle rocking of the lorry, their mood turned quietly euphoric as the miles unwound beneath them.

After a while Lynn's head nodded sideways and her face came to rest against Serge's left shoulder. As the tension of the moment receded, weariness at last took hold. A moment passed and then Serge reached out and put his arm around her. Exactly as it had been before, it seemed to be the most natural thing in the world to be close to him like this now.

'How do you feel?' Lynn whispered without looking up.

'Fine,' he replied. 'How about you?'

She nodded slowly. 'Fine.' And she really meant it, too.

'Sleep now,' he said gently, and stifled a yawn of his own. 'You have looked after me long enough. Now it is my turn to look after you.'

And in his arms, she slept . . .

'Come on, you two — wakey, wakey! End of the line!'

Lynn and Serge snapped awake as the cheerful lorry driver grinned across at them.

'Sorry to disturb you two lovebirds and all that,' he went on with a mischievous chuckle, 'but this is as far as I go.'

Hurriedly — and self-consciously — the two fugitives disentangled themselves from the comfortable position in which they had fallen asleep and hopped down from the cab. It had stopped raining and the sky had lightened perceptibly to show them the sprawling city of Doncaster, which was largely deserted at the moment because it was still quite early on Sunday morning.

They thanked the driver and watched him drive away, refreshed by their brief sleep but still weary. Lynn rubbed her eyes and looked around, then glanced at her watch. It was seven-thirty. Their absence was sure to have been discovered by this time. In London, Ozerov and Miros would have been alerted, and back at the manor, the guards would be combing the countryside for them.

She shuddered, for it was a frightening scenario, but already they had come roughly sixty miles — an encouraging thought to which she was determined to hold.

Turning her attention back to Serge, she asked, 'Are you hungry?'

He smiled fleetingly at her. 'I'm famished.'

That was a good sign, and it pleased her. 'Come on, then. I'm sure we can find a café open somewhere.'

They set off towards the city centre as church bells called the faithful to prayer. To any casual observer they might have been holidaymakers, tourists getting an early start. But as they walked along side by side, Lynn remembered what the lorry driver had called them when he'd woken them up

— lovebirds — and that description seemed to fit them best of all.

They found a small café, went inside and ordered breakfast. Taking a table at the rear of the establishment, they spent a few minutes just luxuriating in the warm, fragrant air and the welcome comfort of the quaint, ladderback chairs, feeling safe at last, and optimistic about the immediate future.

The food came and they ate ravenously, but Lynn sensed that something was troubling her companion, and after she had paid the bill and they were on their way again, he gave voice to it.

'You will think me old-fashioned, I know,' he said haltingly. 'But it — it does not come easily to me, allowing a woman to do so much for me. I am not used to it. To my way of thinking, it should be the other way around. As things are, it makes me feel awkward. Inadequate.'

'Don't give it a second thought, Serge. I haven't.'

'I can't help it,' he replied. Without

warning, he suddenly stopped in the middle of the broad pavement. 'Look — I want you to leave me now, Lynn. Just go.'

She was dumbfounded. 'Go?'

'Yes. Distance yourself from me. You have done enough already — more than enough — but every moment you stay by my side, you put yourself in peril. You know that.'

Still shocked by his outburst, she said, 'I thought we'd already been through all this.'

'And so we have,' he replied earnestly. 'But I have had much time to think since then, and I . . . ' He shook his head. 'I cannot put you in any more danger. You must go and leave me to do what must be done — alone.'

'I can't, Serge. Do you really think I could just put you out of my mind as easily as that?' Realising what she had said, Lynn quickly amended it. 'Do you think I could wash my hands of this entire business so casually — even if I wanted to? And where would I go, anyway? I can hardly go home, can I?'

'You have friends,' he said stubbornly. 'Surely you could stay with them until this affair is settled one way or the other?'

'And put them at risk as well?' This time it was she who shook her head. 'I'm sorry, Serge, but you — you're stuck with me, I'm afraid. And if you'd known me for any length of time, you'd know I can be as stubborn as the best of them when I choose to be.'

He looked at the determination of her stance and expression and smiled.

'I believe you,' he said. 'And I would very much like to know you for a long, long period of time, but — '

Lynn said simply, 'You're not getting rid of me that easily — '

He nodded reluctantly. 'Well, you understand that I had to try, at least.'

'I understand.'

'You really are a remarkable woman, you know,' he said on the spur of the moment.

She looked up at him and grinned.

'Why, thank you.'

'I mean it.'

'I know you — '

Suddenly Lynn's voice cut off and a look of horror twisted her features as she focused on something behind him.

Seeing the change in her expression, Serge asked, 'What . . . ?'

But there was no time to explain. Grabbing him by the hand, Lynn dragged him into the nearest shop, a newsagent's, and they both stared blankly at the display of magazines, keeping their backs to the door as a car cruised past outside.

'What is it?' Serge asked in a whisper.

Lynn was trembling, both inside and out.

'That car,' she said in a quietly urgent voice. 'The one that just went past. I've seen it before — back at the house!'

He blanched. 'Are you sure?'

'You remember I told you I drove into York one day last week? Well, that was the same car that followed me then.'

Serge nodded and said almost to himself, 'We've underestimated them, haven't we? They must have checked on us during the night, found us both missing and put two and two together.'

'But why have they come here, of all places?' Lynn wanted to know. 'We could have gone anywhere.'

Serge thought before responding. 'They must have a pretty good idea where we're going. They've probably come on ahead to stop us if we should manage to get this far.' He eyed her keenly. 'Do you think they spotted us?'

She shook her head. 'No. I'm almost certain I recognised them first.'

'Well, thank goodness for that.'

Behind them, the newsagent cleared his throat noisily. 'Are you going to buy something, or what?' he demanded at last. 'This is a paper shop, you know, not a conference centre.'

Lynn and Serge turned around to face him. Lynn spotted a pocket guide to Britain in a rack on the counter and said, 'I'll take one of these, please.'

She paid for the book and, together, she and Serge stepped carefully back into the street, their eyes constantly swivelling in every direction.

The road was empty of traffic now, but the danger that they might cross paths with their pursuers again unless they moved on quickly refused to go away.

'Where to now?' Serge asked urgently.

Remembering what she had read in the local guidebook earlier, Lynn replied, 'There's a water bus service that plies the South Yorkshire Canal not far from here. It'll be the last form of transport Ozerov's men will be expecting us to take.'

He nodded. 'You're right, as always.'

'Come on, then.'

Forcing themselves to keep to a casual pace that would not attract unwelcome attention, they began to follow the signs for Hexthorpe, which lay about a mile away. A thought suddenly occurred to Lynn, and she told Serge to put his arm around her.

'What?'

'Those guards,' she explained in an undertone, 'are looking for two people, not a couple. There's a difference, you know.'

Seeing her logic, he put his arm around her shoulders and she snaked an arm around his waist, and immediately the shape of them, the shape their pursuers would be looking for, altered. All at once their resemblance to relaxed holidaymakers increased, and from a distance at least, they looked nothing like the desperate runaways they were.

★   ★   ★

They left the city proper without spotting the blue car again. Lynn tried to tell herself that maybe she had never really seen it in the first place, that it had only been a figment of her overtired imagination, but she knew that she *had* seen it, and the knowledge made goosebumps rise on her skin.

Finally a group of farm buildings came into sight. They followed them down to the canal's edge and picked up the water bus at a nearby jetty.

Lynn bought tickets for Conisbrough, which was the last stop on the eight-mile route. It was still fairly early and they were practically the only passengers on the sleek vessel.

At last the water bus growled to life and pushed away from the jetty to chug and sway south along the contortions of the picturesque canal.

They felt the tension ebbing out of them again. Serge noticed Lynn's hands fidgeting in her lap and reached over to cover them with one of his own. Their eyes met. Hers were frightened, his full of strength and understanding.

'We'll be all right now,' he assured her. 'As long as we keep doing the last thing they expect, we'll make it.'

'But if we're right, and they've already guessed where we're going, what's to stop them from calling off the signing of the agreement on Tuesday, postponing it until they've recaptured us?'

The lines of Serge's face suddenly hardened as he thought about the traitors and their betrayal of him.

'They won't postpone it,' he said confidently. 'They can't, not easily. Representatives of your heads of state will be present, as will high-ranking members of your government. You do not make your excuses to people of their standing and hope they will come back again next week. Besides, I know Ozerov and Miros. They are confident men. Some might say over-confident. They are certain they will have caught us by Tuesday.' His grey eyes returned to her face and softened again. 'But they don't know us, do they?'

'No,' she murmured. 'They don't.'

They fell silent again, as Serge looked out of the window. The canal was filled with atmosphere and history. For two centuries it had been used to transport coal and steel. Now it was a true beauty spot, given over to recreation and pleasure.

'What are you thinking about?' Lynn asked.

He smiled at her. 'About everything that has happened to me in the last two weeks,' he replied. 'And especially the last few days. It — it all seems more like a dream, really. A nightmare, some of it, but shall I tell you the craziest part of it all?'

She nodded, and he said sincerely, 'I wouldn't have missed it for anything, because meeting you has made it all worthwhile.'

The water bus sliced through the dull, green water and passed under a disused railway bridge. They were suddenly plunged into brief, intimate darkness. In that moment, each heard the heaviness of the other's breathing, suddenly became aware of a closeness that went beyond the physical.

Unhurriedly then, Serge leaned forward to touch his lips to hers. When Lynn made no attempt to shy away, he grew bolder, reached up, ran his long fingers through her luxuriant, blonde hair, then cupped the back of her head and kissed her with more fervour.

It was a tender meeting of lips, a gentle but insistent pressure, a string of little, loving kisses that eventually built into one big kiss that fanned fires in each of them.

Then daylight spilled back into the water bus and they slowly broke apart, the eyes of each moving over the other's face, searching for something that would let them know that their kiss had been right or wrong, that the feelings they had, or thought they had, for each other were real and not imagined.

Lynn looked away from his searching gaze, unsure how she should react. She felt confused, scared even, but scared by the potency of her own emotions for him, and scared that she might make a fool of herself. After all, how could this be love? And even if it was, where could any relationship between them really go? They were separated by an unbridgeable divide. They were from different backgrounds, different walks of life. They had nothing in common, she told herself harshly, save that both their lives were being threatened by the same evil men.

She felt his eyes on her, but refused to look back at him. No — as sure as she was that she loved him, she knew she must not give in to her desires and emotions. This was an extraordinary period of her life. It was only to be expected that their heightened emotions would deceive them. They were living every moment as if it might be their last, after all. It was only natural that they should try to encapsulate all of life's rich experiences into whatever time remained to them.

'Lynn?'

At last Lynn turned back to face him. Pain showed in his eyes, regret for what he had done because he believed that his actions had been unwelcome and upsetting to her.

Lynn got the guidebook out, cleared

her throat and said in a businesslike tone, 'Come on — we'd better see where we go from Conisbrough.'

Something in his eyes died, and he nodded with sad acceptance.

6

The water bus ploughed on through a limestone quarry and stopped for a while until a lock could be negotiated. Then it chugged on until a magnificent castle thrust up from a vast belt of trees ahead to signify journey's end.

The remainder of the short trip had been spent in an awkward, wretched silence. Lynn could tell that Serge regretted having kissed her, and she wanted to tell him not to, because it was the one thing she had wanted him to do very much.

At the same time, utterly convinced that their relationship could go nowhere and might only lead to more heartache in the long run, she didn't want to talk about it anymore. Anything she said now would only hurt his feelings, and she dearly did not want to do that.

So she remained silent, and the

silence was awful and oppressive, but there was no help for it. In any case, everything they were going through now would cease to be of any real importance on Tuesday. By then Serge would once again have the fortunes of his country to concern him, if luck was with them . . . and if it wasn't, they would both find themselves under lock and key back at the manor, facing a short, bleak future.

Lingering on the grassy towpath beside the jetty while they got their bearings, they watched the water bus fill with passengers bound for Doncaster, and waited until the boat began to surge back the way it had come. When it was gone and the jetty and towpath were once again deserted, they set off along a narrow, rutted track that led on towards the heart of the town.

The day was shaping up to be bright and breezy, with the occasional dark cloud threatening more rain for later, but the isolated manor from which they had made their escape just twelve hours earlier was receding farther and farther with every step they took, and that was a cheering thought.

'Lynn,' Serge said at last, his voice halting and embarrassed. 'Lynn, I owe you an apology. I — '

Without looking at him, Lynn said, 'Please, Serge. I don't want to talk about it just now.'

He nodded. 'All right, but as long as you know, I apologise for my behaviour. I did not mean to take advantage of you. I — I'll not forget myself again.'

Making no reply, Lynn concentrated on their surroundings. They were just passing a gap in the tall hedge that screened a near-deserted carpark from the bustling main road sixty yards away. And it was at exactly that moment that a new voice spoke up behind them, in Russian.

'That's far enough, Varda.'

Breaking stride and twisting at the waist, Lynn and Serge noticed two things in rapid succession — the same distinctive blue car that Lynn had spotted in Doncaster, now practically the only vehicle in the carpark . . . and a scowling guard who had spent much of his time in the gatehouse back at the manor.

And to make the matter even worse — the guard was holding a small, black pistol in his fist.

There was a moment of complete, stunned surprise. Then, without having to be told, Serge raised his hands and stepped protectively in front of Lynn, screening her from the firearm.

'Surprised to see me?' the guard asked. He was a brawny man with a boxer's face and a low stubble of dark hair shading his bullet head. He was perhaps forty, muscular but in no way unusual — save for the gun in his big, veined hand. He was dressed in a creased grey suit and a stiff white shirt. His black tie was a funereal slash down the front of his barrel chest.

Hesitantly, Serge said, 'It's Lanik, isn't it? Piotr Lanik?'

The gunman nodded.

'You used to be one of my most faithful guards, Piotr,' he continued, his voice echoing the regret he felt.

'That is true, but now our rôles have changed. Now it is you who are the slave, and I am the master.'

Serge gave him a searching look. 'Is that what Ozerov has told you? Filled your head with lies like that? We were never slaves and masters, Lanik. You know that. We were simply countrymen struggling together, side by side, for the good of all.'

Lanik gestured with the gun. 'I have no time to argue about it. No time, and no desire. Now turn around, the pair of you. And no trouble. First I'm going to cuff your hands behind your backs to make sure you cause no more disruption. Then I want you to get into the car.'

Stalling for time, Serge said, 'How — how did you find us, Piotr? This is a big country by our standards. How did you know to find us here?'

Lanik looked both ways along the

track, and relaxed a little when he saw that they were all alone and with little immediate prospect of being interrupted.

Submitting to vanity, he said, 'We didn't know where to find you, not for certain. But when it became obvious that you had not gone directly to the authorities in York, Mr Ozerov realised that you would most likely head straight for our embassy in London, perhaps with the intention of wrecking or otherwise sabotaging Tuesday's assembly. After that, it was just a matter of putting ourselves in your position, trying to think the way you would think.'

He gave a nasty chuckle. 'And it has paid off, hasn't it? We have spread ourselves thinly, it is true, but Mr Ozerov has a man at every rail, coach and bus station you would be most likely to use. It was my good fortune to be posted here — my distinction to be the one to recapture you.'

Suddenly his face darkened and he

jerked the gun again, making Lynn gasp.

'Now — turn around!'

Still Serge disobeyed him. 'Or what, Piotr? Do you really expect me to believe that you will use that gun? Here? In broad daylight? With half the good people of this town just the other side of this carpark?'

Lanik's fingers flexed around the handle of the gun. 'I'm warning you . . . '

Incredibly, Serge ignored him and closed the distance between them by one measured step. Slightly cowed by his courage, Lanik retreated a pace until the backs of his legs leaned against the side of the car.

'I mean it,' he hissed.

In a cool, unnerving voice, Serge said, 'I don't think you do, Piotr. As much as anything else, Ozerov wants me unmarked, doesn't he — until the time comes for my 'assassination,' that is.'

Lynn whispered, 'Serge . . . ' Then,

louder, 'Be careful, Serge . . . '

But suddenly it was as if Serge was without fear, for he continued to advance upon Lanik, calling his bluff, almost daring him to use the weapon.

Lynn watched through disbelieving eyes, her head shaking slowly from side to side, expecting at any moment to hear the crack of a gunshot and see the man she loved hunch up and then collapse . . .

The man she loved . . .

All at once the true urgency of the situation grabbed her and his name welled up in her throat almost like a scream. 'Serge!'

The sound and desperation of that one word took them all by surprise, and the moment Serge saw Lanik's watery blue eyes turn in Lynn's direction, he threw caution to the wind and lunged forward, his right fist a swiping blur.

Lanik grunted and dropped like a stone at Serge's feet. Serge immediately bent and snatched up the bully's fallen weapon, but Lanik had no further use for it. He was unconscious.

As if by magic, Lynn appeared at Serge's side, grabbing for him, hugging him tearfully, just grateful that no harm had come to him, that he was still alive.

'Oh, Serge,' she breathed, holding him close and burying her face in his heaving chest. 'Thank goodness you're all right. If anything had happened to you . . . '

He reached for her and gently eased her back to arm's length, the better to examine her. She saw that his face was covered in a fine sheen of perspiration, and that he was showing surprise at the intensity of her reaction.

'That was either the bravest thing I've ever seen, or the most foolish!' she said, and she sort of chuckled and sobbed all in one, and dashed tears from her eyes with the back of one hand.

He grinned crookedly at her, then shook his numb right hand to get some feeling back into it.

'You're right again,' he agreed, then

sobered. 'But we can't hang around here.' He indicated the car with a jerk of his chin. 'Think you can drive this?'

She nodded gamely.

'All right.' He bent, went through Lanik's pockets, found the keys and handed them to her. Then he discovered a set of handcuffs as well.

Reaching a decision, he said, 'Poor old Piotr. When he wakes up, he's going to find himself cuffed to the sturdiest bush in this carpark. Not very sporting of me, I know — but at least it will buy us enough time to get far away from here.' Quite unexpectedly, another grin split his rugged face. 'I wonder how he will explain his predicament to the police when they arrive?'

He took Lanik under the arms and dragged him out of sight. Lynn got into the car and quickly familiarised herself with the layout of the dashboard. When Serge came back and climbed in beside her, she switched on the engine and drove them out of the carpark and on to the road for Rotherham.

★ ★ ★

At last they were really moving, and feeling buoyed up at having outwitted their pursuers yet again. Rotherham lay no more than six or seven miles away. Beyond that came Sheffield, and from there the M1 took them ever south.

The day wore on and as the clouds bulked tighter together, it grew darker. They stopped at a service station in the late afternoon, and cleaned and tidied themselves up in the restrooms. Then Serge filled the petrol tank while Lynn went to buy some sandwiches and cups of tea.

But it was an all-too-brief respite. They were both living on their nerves and in dire need of proper rest, but they had to keep on the move. They had no choice. A clock was ticking. There was a deadline to meet — a showdown to be faced in London.

Darkness fell. Glaring headlights danced across the rainswept windscreen in sweeping yellow arcs. Finally Lynn shook her head and said, 'It's no good, Serge. I've got to pull over for a while. I'm almost falling asleep at the wheel.'

They came to a slip road and followed it through the murky night until the motorway lay behind them and a quiet, leafy lane appeared ahead. Lynn steered the car on to a grassy verge and then parked. Suddenly all was silent but for the tiny pitter-patter of rain dancing on the roof and against the windows.

Serge peered out into the darkness, then said, 'Not another light in sight anywhere. We should be safe enough here until morning.'

Lynn put her head back against the rest and closed her aching eyes. 'Well, that's something,' she groaned, 'I know it sounds like a cliché, but I'm so tired I think I could sleep for a week.'

'Well,' he allowed, 'one way or another, it's been quite a day.'

'How does your hand feel?'

Serge flexed it. 'Better than poor Piotr's jaw,' he joked grimly.

'You took a terrible risk though, Serge. If that man had pulled the trigger — ' She shuddered and lowered her head, unable to carry on.

'But he didn't,' he said softly. He looked through the rain-pebbled windscreen and said, 'I really am sorry, Lynn. For earlier, I mean. I know I had no right to do what I did — '

'Please, Serge. Forget it.'

He was quiet for a time.

'Do you have someone else? Is that it?' he asked apprehensively.

'No. There's no-one.'

He nodded, almost to himself.

'It is the same with me. Or rather, it was. Until I met you.'

She made a disparaging sound in her throat that was meant to discourage him.

'You don't really mean that, Serge. You might think you do, but — well, the pressure we've both been under ever since Friday night . . . '

'Do you really believe that?' he asked.

'Well, what else should I believe?' she

snapped. Then she moderated her tone. 'Look, I — I like you, Serge. You know I do. I care for you, very much. But . . . ' She shook her head. 'There's still so much uncertainty. There's no telling what might happen between here and London. Perhaps afterwards, if it all works out, we could be . . . friends.'

'You must know that I want more than that — for both of us.'

Steeling herself to say what must be said, she murmured, 'Please don't think I'm doubting your sincerity. If you must know, I think you are the kindest and most gentle man I've ever met. But I also believe that you're confusing love — or something like it — with . . . ' She searched for the right word. 'I don't know — gratitude.'

She could feel the words striking him like blows, and hated herself for voicing them, but as unpleasant as the task was, she knew they had to be said.

He fell silent again. Then he turned and examined her profile in the rainwashed darkness and said, 'You know I'm not confusing anything, Lynn. You know it. But I accept one thing. There is much uncertainty in our lives at present, and I have no desire to add any more. So I will say nothing else of my feelings, for now. But when this is all behind us, I will tell you again how I feel about you, how I know I feel. And then it will be up to you to tell me how you feel.'

Lynn looked out into the stormy night and thought about the men who were out there even now, relentlessly hunting them down.

She shivered.

★   ★   ★

When Lynn finally fell asleep, her rest was tormented by images of Piotr Lanik and his deadly black pistol, Mr Ozerov and Dr Miros with their cunning smiles and treacherous ways — and then the simple, complete sincerity of the man beside her — Duke Serge Varda.

But even as she thought of his title, so she was reminded of one of the main barriers that would always exist between them. Out here, in the middle of nowhere, they were equals, facing and fighting against the same threat in the same way. But when the threat was gone, and the fight was over, what would be left save memories? He would go back to his title, his country and his heritage. She would return to her life as an agency nurse — and that would be that.

She was not unhappy with her life as it had been, but she knew that it would seem an emptier and more hollow place when she and Serge were once more separated by that unbridgeable divide.

The rain stopped shortly after midnight. Then came the steady drip and splash as the last of it tumbled from branches and leaves to puddle in the shiny grass. Lynn, at best only managing an unsettled sort of doze, was aware of it all until about four o'clock, when she finally fell into a deep, undisturbed slumber.

Sometime around eight o'clock, she opened her eyes and winced at the sudden blaze of sunshine that greeted her. She sat up straighter, the small of her back protesting at the uncomfortable sitting position in which she had spent the night.

She leaned forward, rubbed her face to chase away the last vestiges of sleep, and quickly finger-combed her blonde hair into some semblance of order.

Catching sight of her reflection in the rear-view mirror, she saw the combination of tension and strain that tightened her face and wondered what Serge had ever seen in her. But then, sourly, she reminded herself of their circumstances, and the fact that he hadn't seen anything, not really. His situation had been so hopeless that he had needed to find at least one ray of hope, even the faintest promise of possible happiness to boost his morale and bolster his resolve.

She was convinced that love didn't really come into it, at least not for Serge, but the need to love most certainly did — and they were two completely different things.

Coming out of her reverie, she suddenly realised with a start that she was all alone in the car. When she looked beyond the passenger-side window, however, she saw Serge leaning against a thick, knotted tree about twenty feet away, his shoulders rising and falling to the motion of his quickened breathing, and she quickly got out of the car and rushed to join him.

The morning was misty and quiet, apart from the pleasant background chorus of birdsong. Lynn hurried through the dew-damp grass, and when he heard her coming, he turned to face her.

She saw at once by the pallor of his skin and the beads of perspiration that mottled his forehead, that he still hadn't entirely managed to shake off the after-effects of the lethal sedatives he'd been given, and although he tried to make light of it, she could see that he was only clinging to consciousness by the sheer, unyielding tenacity of his will.

'How long have you been standing out here like this?' she asked anxiously, feeling the dampness of his clothes as she helped to support his weight. 'You're chilled to the bone.'

He shook his head. 'I — I'm all right. It's just — I feel so weak. I thought maybe some fresh air . . . '

'Come on, back to the car and rest for a moment,' she counselled patiently. 'I'm not really sure where we are, but I'll see what's at the end of this lane. Maybe there's a shop, or something, where I can buy us something to eat. That should help a bit.'

He allowed her to guide him back to the car, angered by his own helplessness, and when he was settled, Lynn took her bag and followed the deserted lane down towards a small cluster of cottages at the foot of a steep incline.

Twenty minutes later she came back with some pre-packed sandwiches and soft drinks, and he forced himself to eat even though his appetite had temporarily deserted him. Slowly the mist burned off and the sky showed through as a clear, cloudless blue.

'How do you feel now?' Lynn asked sometime later, reaching out to take his pulse, which was steady and settled again, and then putting the back of her hand to his forehead to confirm that he was no longer feverish.

'Better,' he said huskily.

'I've been thinking,' she said. 'We're going to have to hire another car. We can't drive all the way to London in this one. Ozerov's men will be on the lookout for it.' She gestured towards the distant cottages. 'There's a little car rental place next door to the garage down there. Do you think you can walk that far?'

He nodded and reached for the door handle.

'I can do it,' he replied doggedly.

His strength started coming back as they strode down the peaceful lane and into the anonymous village. A middle-aged woman was just unlocking the car rental office as they approached, and after a while Lynn had filled in a request form and handed it over, together with her credit card.

A short time later she was given the keys to a neat, silver Maestro that was sitting on the garage forecourt, fuelled up and ready to go. She and Serge climbed inside and Lynn switched on the engine.

'Well,' she said with an uncertain little smile. 'This is it, Serge. The last leg of the trip. By this time tomorrow, we'll know if we've failed or succeeded.'

He looked straight ahead, his mind busy with thoughts of his country and what the price of failure would mean for his countrymen.

'You're still determined to see this through to the end?' he questioned.

She nodded.

Iron resolve came into the set of his

jaw. 'Then let's do it,' he said quietly.

She put her foot on the accelerator and they left this village behind them.

★ ★ ★

The motorway was an endless concrete treadmill that drew them ever closer to their destiny. As the clock turned steadily to chalk up the miles, Chester-field, then Nottingham, then Leicester all fell behind them, and Rugby, then Northampton, beckoned ahead.

Morning pushed towards noon. They left the M1 and switched on to the A428. Mostly they drove in silence, except for once, when Lynn began to feel uneasy about a car that appeared to be following them.

Serge threw a look over one shoulder, then shook his head to dispel her misgivings. 'No,' he said gravely. 'In any case, Ozerov will have called off any pursuit by this time. They will not come after us now. They know where we are going. They know when we plan to get there — so now they will wait for us to come to them.'

'You're doing nothing to make me feel any easier about all this, you know,' Lynn said, ruefully.

That quirky smile worked across his face again. 'I'm sorry, but it's as well to be prepared.'

'Uh, talking of which — ' she began.

'Yes?'

'What are we going to do when we get to London?' she asked directly.

Serge stared ahead through the windscreen. 'I've thought about little else.'

'And?'

'Security at my embassy will be as tight as a drum tomorrow. We won't even be able to get close to the place. So we must get into the building tonight instead. And once we're inside, we must find somewhere to hide until morning.'

With gallows humour, Lynn noted, 'Oh, that's all, is it? Should be easy.'

'Actually, it might not be as difficult

as it sounds,' he replied with a sideways glance at her. 'There's a staff entrance at the rear of the building with a computerised lock. All we have to do is key in the right combination and the door will open automatically.'

'And you know the combination?'

He winced. 'Well, yes . . . I think so, but if I get it wrong . . . '

'Yes?' she said questioningly.

'An alarm will be triggered. Unless we get away quickly, we may find ourselves surrounded by embassy guards — and under arrest.'

Bedford came and went. The afternoon began its slide towards early evening. The miles continued to multiply. Eventually they transferred on to the A6, and after that, London swallowed them whole.

By that time, early evening was darkening the sky over the city, and rush-hour traffic was chaotic. While they were still on the outskirts of the metropolis, they found a place to park and went in search of somewhere to eat and freshen up once again.

The day's driving, coupled with the growing tension, had taken a heavy toll on Lynn. Her eyes felt sore and she had a slight headache, but she knew that she would feel better after something to eat — even though she wasn't especially hungry. Serge, too, looked strained.

As they made their way back to the hire car an hour later, Lynn's hand somehow found its way into his, because the need for consolation and encouragement was strong in each of them now, stronger even than Lynn's determination to keep their relationship on a strictly businesslike footing.

Finally, evening turned to night. The roads emptied of traffic. Pedestrians grew fewer. With tight, dry throats, the two fugitives buckled their seat-belts and Lynn drove them slowly towards the centre of London, where the embassy was located. They parked a little way off from their destination, then got out and walked the rest of the way.

At last the embassy building loomed ahead. A flag snapped briskly in the cool night wind. By mutual consent, they stopped and studied the imposing structure. Lights glowed starkly at practically every window.

Serge glanced down at his lovely companion. 'Come on,' he said. 'As I recall, the River Thames is not far from here. Let's take a moonlit stroll.'

'And then?' she prompted softly.

'And then,' he said, 'with any luck, this place will be in complete darkness, and we can break inside.'

7

In twos and threes, the embassy staff left the building and began their journeys home. At last the final light went out and the building was thrown into darkness, save for the lights that still showed in the main reception beyond the heavy glass doors, and the odd couple that made windows glow along the top floor.

'That's where the traitors will be spending the night,' Serge murmured, pointing towards them. 'The entire top floor is reserved for visiting dignitaries or members of staff who need to stay over. It's more like a hotel up there than an office block.'

Lingering in the shadows of a corner a hundred yards away, Lynn looked at her watch. It was half-past midnight. Tuesday — maybe the most fateful Tuesday of her entire life — was already

160

thirty minutes old.

Still she and Serge forced themselves to wait another half-hour before working their way down to a poorly-lit alley-way that fetched out on to the rear of the building.

The night was dark and quiet. In the distance, traffic-sounds still carried on the wind. Hand in hand, they crept as far as the staff entrance Serge had mentioned earlier, and he bent to study the numbers on the small, metallic pad that would, if pressed correctly, allow them to enter.

Bending beside him and putting a hand on his shoulder, Lynn whispered urgently, 'Are you sure you know the right combination?'

He made no immediate reply, but then said, almost to himself, 'It's a seven-number sequence. I'm pretty sure about the first six numbers, but . . . '

Cautiously he pressed one of the buttons, then a second, a third and so on. He hesitated then, rubbing his index finger against his thumb, unwilling to commit himself to the all-important seventh digit.

'It's either a four or a five,' he hissed.

'And you're not certain which?'

He glanced around at her. 'I'm afraid that you're guess is going to be as good as mine.'

The wind picked up and blew a discarded newspaper along the narrow thoroughfare towards them. To their already-strained nerves it sounded loud and distracting.

Turning his attention back to the pad, Serge whispered, 'I think it's four. I'm going to press four. But get ready to run, just in case I'm wrong.'

His finger hovered over the button, but he held back from pressing it.

Impulsively, Lynn said, 'Press five.'

'What?'

'I've just got a feeling, that's all.'

'And I've just convinced myself that it's four.'

'Well, if you're sure . . . '

He made no reply, but drawing in a deep breath, he finally pressed down on the pad and his finger depressed the number five button.

The door clicked open.

Lynn felt Serge sag beneath her hand, but when he rose back to his full, generous height, he was grinning tightly.

'I take back everything I ever said about women's intuition,' he muttered.

He pushed the door wider and they went inside and closed it behind them. They found themselves in a short, confined passage, at the far end of which lay an old, wrought-iron circular staircase, an open doorway that apparently descended into a shadowy basement, and the shining doors of an elevator.

Quickly they reached the end of the passage. Lynn gestured to the basement, but Serge shook his head.

'No. Ozerov's bound to order a thorough search of the building tomorrow morning, and the basement's one of the first places the guards will check. We need somewhere else to hide, somewhere less obvious. Come on.'

He led Lynn over to the rickety staircase and they began to ascend as quietly as they could.

'The attic's our best bet,' Serge whispered over his shoulder. 'It's big, crammed with junk and there are plenty of places to hide.'

They reached the first floor without event, and Serge went over to a set of double doors and peered cautiously through one small, square window at the darkened corridor and now-silent offices that lay beyond. Then he came back, took Lynn's hand and almost before she knew it, they were climbing higher through the dark, deserted silence.

'Do you still think your plan to expose the traitors can work, Serge?' Lynn asked in a worried undertone.

'It has to,' he replied, without looking around.

'But surely it would be safe to go to the police now?'

He paused for a moment, and turned

back to her. 'Maybe it would,' he replied softly, after a moment. 'But there is something else you must understand, Lynn. My country is a small and seemingly insignificant one. For my people, every day is a struggle just to survive. They have hardly any hope left, and precious little self-esteem. But if I could strike a blow against their enemies and be seen to do so, if I can expose them by my own actions, think how that would inspire them, Lynn! Think what it could do to give them back some of their self-worth!'

Lynn came closer to him and looked up at him with tears sparkling in her eyes.

'You are a very brave and selfless man, Serge,' she whispered sincerely. 'You will be good for your country. I know it.'

'And we could be good for each other,' he replied quietly. 'You know that as well, don't you?'

She looked away from him. 'Come

on,' she urged, suddenly brisk. 'We've got to find somewhere to hide.'

The second floor was a carbon copy of the first, and the third was a carbon copy of the second. As they reached the fourth, however, they heard a jumble of conversation coming from somewhere beyond the double doors, and they instinctively fell into a crouch, there against the cold, black iron.

Light was fanning out through the windows in the doors, and sending huge shadows stretching up the walls. The voices, coming from someplace farther along the corridor, were distorted and muffled by distance. When it became obvious that they were in no immediate danger, however, Serge lifted out of his crouch and together, he and Lynn tiptoed up to the doors.

Serge chanced a brief look around the edge of the nearest pane of glass, then drew back and indicated that Lynn should take a look for herself.

She did so, and quickly sucked in a startled gasp.

The long corridor on the other side of the glass was brightly lit and thickly carpeted. Potted plants sat on ornate pedestals outside delicately-painted doors. As Serge had said, the top floor of the embassy more closely resembled a hotel than an office block.

What had taken Lynn's attention, most of all, was a group of men who were conversing outside one of the doors mid-way along the corridor — Mr Ozerov, Dr Miros, and the man she had seen that night back at the manor — Serge's double.

Quickly she pulled back into the darkness and stared at her companion, whose shadowy face had now turned grim.

He leaned forward and took another look along the corridor. She watched as he shook his head in wonder, and when he also drew back, she heard him mutter, 'It really is a remarkable likeness, isn't it?'

One of the plotters voiced a name — Lynn's. With renewed interest, Serge put his ear to the gap between the doors and tried to hear more. Suddenly he and Lynn found themselves in close proximity.

Lynn saw Serge's lip curl, and then there were footsteps and they both looked through the glass just as Ozerov and Miros walked off down the corridor and the man who looked so much like Serge let himself into the room outside which they had all just been conversing.

Blending back into the darkness, Lynn asked Serge what they had been saying.

'It seems that my double has been getting a little anxious,' Serge whispered. 'Ozerov and Miros were trying to calm him down and assure him that everything will be all right. They told him they have men out everywhere, searching for us. They say we'll never get within a mile of this place. They've told him to get some sleep, and that they'll arrange for someone to bring him a nightcap to help him relax.'

As Lynn digested all that, Serge squinted off into the darkness. When he turned his face back to her, she saw something new in his expression and asked, 'What is it? What's the matter?'

His smile was a surprisingly roguish thing. 'I've just had an idea,' he whispered. 'I think I know exactly how we're going to unmask those traitors.'

And without further ado, he told her what was in his mind.

When he was finished, a look of horror had come into Lynn's face. 'You can't, Serge!' she whispered insistently. 'You'd never get away with it!'

In that cool way of his, he said, 'There's only one way to find out.'

'But it's too dangerous!'

'Listen to me, Lynn. Everything about this entire episode has been dangerous so far. Whatever plan we concoct is bound to have its risks.'

'But this — '

He held her arms in a firm yet gentle grip. 'Don't you remember what we said yesterday? As long as we do the last thing Ozerov expects, we'll be all right. Well, you have to admit, this is the last thing he'll be expecting.'

She wanted to dissuade him from taking such a foolhardy course, but she could see that his mind was made up. His fingers tightened on her in a reassuring squeeze. 'No more arguing now. We need to get started.'

He put his face back to the glass and checked to make sure that the corridor was still empty. Then he pushed the doors open and together he and Lynn went through and ran as lightly as they could down to the room into which Serge's double had retired.

When they got there, Serge cleared his throat and rapped on the door. A voice on the other side asked irritably, 'What is it now?'

Keeping his eyes on Lynn, Serge said in a subservient tone, 'Your drink, sir.'

They heard footsteps crossing the floor and prepared themselves. The door swung open. Serge's double, in his shirtsleeves now, and with his tie loosened at the neck, said, 'Just put it down on — '

Then he realised exactly whom he was addressing, and his grey eyes widened, his jaw dropped and blood drained from his face.

But his surprise was only temporary, and almost at once a cunning that Serge himself could never possess came into his eyes and his lips began to form into a yell of warning.

Serge saw it coming and shoved his double back into the room hard enough to wind him. He and Lynn both rushed inside after him and Lynn hurriedly closed the door. Meanwhile, with desperation lending him courage, Serge's double threw himself at the very man he was here to imperson-ate — and ruin — but again Serge retaliated, and the double fell back on to the bed, holding his jaw and breathing hard.

Serge drew out the little, black pistol he'd taken from Piotr Lanik and pointed it at his mirror image. He had

171

no intention of actually using it, but his double wasn't to know that. At once the man on the mattress froze, his frightened eyes going wide again.

'Please, you have to believe me! They forced me to — ' he babbled.

'Not a sound,' Serge warned sharply, and his double promptly fell silent, his face screwing up now as the gun in Serge's rock-steady grip menaced him.

Lynn scanned the room. It was of average size, and divided by the nature of its furniture into part bedroom and part sitting-room. Curtains were drawn against the night, and low light came from a fluorescent strip over the bed. A door in the facing wall led through to a small bathroom. Lynn crossed over to it and checked to make sure it was empty.

Now the man on the bed began to whine. 'Please — you must let me talk. Give you my side of the story . . . '

Serge's glance was withering. 'Enough of your lies,' he gritted. 'All I want from you now is the truth, my friend. Give me the truth and it may just go in your

172

favour when all of this is over.'

Willing to clutch at any straw now, the duke's look-alike bobbed his head anxiously. 'Anything! Anything!'

'You have a name?'

'Yes. Jan — Jan Korvis.'

'And who are you, Korvis? Apart from my double, that is?'

Under questioning, Korvis revealed that he was an unemployed actor who had been recruited by Ozerov and Miros several months earlier. Impoverished just like most of his countrymen, Korvis confessed that he had been tempted by promises of wealth and position. He insisted that Ozerov had forced him to play the part he had been given, but neither Serge nor Lynn believed him. Korvis was all too obviously another of those men whom greed had corrupted completely.

But the actor's admission did raise another question.

'This 'part' you mentioned,' Serge prodded. 'What exactly does it entail?'

As Serge had suspected, Korvis was

to portray him in a most unflattering light — to be rude and arrogant, pedantic and difficult — and finally to refuse point-blank to have anything to do with the trade agreement. When pictures of such behaviour were beamed back to their country, Serge's people would feel betrayed by their duke and Ozerov's agents would then go to work fanning their discontent until it became fully-fledged rebellion.

Lynn swallowed softly. So — Serge had been right about everything. She released her breath in a low hiss, feeling disgust well up inside her as she remembered all the smiles and lies of the men who had employed her in the first place.

Suddenly there was a knock at the door. About to say more, Korvis fell silent and stared up at Serge. Lynn looked at him, too, suddenly rooted to the spot. Then, as she saw Serge glance swiftly around the room and sensed the quick workings of his agile mind, she saw why he was and would continue to be the best chance of a prosperous future his country possessed, and all at once she felt another wave of love and admiration for him that was almost too much to bear.

Serge thought for a moment, then passed the gun to Lynn.

'Quick,' he told Korvis in an undertone as he stripped off his jacket and sweater. 'Into the bathroom with you, my friend. Not a sound out of you, and no tricks. This fine lady is as desperate as I, and with a gun she never misses her target. Do I make myself clear?'

Still thoroughly frightened and eager to please, Korvis nodded quickly.

Again there was a knock at the door. Serge met Lynn's eyes as Korvis got up and headed for the bathroom, and he mouthed a question.

'Will you be all right?'

Lynn nodded, finding strength in this tall, regal man, then followed Korvis out of sight. Serge quickly smoothed down his hair, then cleared his throat and opened the door.

'Yes?' he asked in a surly tone.

An embassy employee was standing in the corridor, a tray upon which sat a tumbler filled with a measure of whisky in his hands. 'I was told — '

'Yes, yes,' Serge said with an irritable wave of one hand. 'Put it over there on the table.'

He stood to one side and waited while the newcomer did as he had been told. The man then turned and asked if that would be all. Serge told him that it would, then closed the door after him, wondering if he had given a convincing enough performance of himself — or rather, of Korvis's impression of himself.

He released his breath in a long sigh, then wiped his brow and went over to the bathroom. When he opened the door, he found Korvis standing in the shower, facing the wall with his hands folded on top of his head, and he couldn't suppress a sudden smile.

'You don't believe in taking any

chances, do you?' he asked fondly.

Relieved to have him back, Lynn grinned self-consciously. 'Give me a few years and I might just get used to all this subterfuge.'

He took the gun back, threw her a heartening wink, then said, 'All right, Korvis, you can turn around now — but keep your hands right where they are.'

Korvis did as he was told.

Serge said tightly, 'How many of the embassy staff are involved in this little deception of yours? The truth, now.'

'Not many,' Korvis replied. 'Mr Ozerov was always determined to keep the numbers small. Less chance that things would go wrong, he said.'

That was good news. Glancing down at Lynn, Serge then returned his eyes to his double. 'Co-operate with us now and we might be able to come to some arrangement with you, Korvis.'

'Of course. Anything!'

'You strike me as quite a talker, Korvis, and that is good. Because I want to hear all about it — everything you have been told to do during your impersonation of me, and everything that is to happen at the signing later today.'

Korvis frowned. 'Everything? But — but why?'

'Because,' Serge said, 'as of now, I am the actor here. And from now on, the part I will be playing is you, Korvis, you playing me.'

★   ★   ★

Once the questioning was finished, and Korvis had talked himself hoarse, Serge bound him hand and foot with flex taken from a bedside lamp, and gagged him with a handkerchief. Leaving him hidden away in the bathroom, the two fugitives then shuffled back into the main room, at once both exhausted and jumpy.

Too tired for further talk, and realising that, for the time being at least, everything that could be said had been said, Serge checked idly through the clothes in the wardrobe while Lynn went across to the window and drew back the curtain.

The city's uneven silhouette broke the dark skyline. Even now, in the middle of the night, London was ablaze with light. She sighed quietly, feeling worried for Serge and concerned by the dangerous game he had elected to play. She didn't want to think about the consequences if it all went wrong. She couldn't bear the thought of life without the man she loved.

And yet, that was precisely what she would have to get used to, because win or lose, they would probably never see each other again after this.

She hugged herself as a sudden shiver ran through her, and told herself that maybe that would be for the best. It would be embarrassing in the extreme for both of them, after all — embarrassing for Serge because he would finally have to concede that he didn't love her as he had believed, and embarrassing for her because she did love him.

She listened to the sounds he made in the bathroom as he began to wash and shave and prepare to assume Korvis's rôle, and wondered if she could ever forget him. She knew she could not. Truly she had never known a kinder, braver or more gentle soul.

She went to a chair in the corner and sat down. It had been so long since her life had been anything like normal that she wondered whether normality would ever return to it.

All that remained now was the business of waiting. She closed her eyes, but somehow felt beyond sleep. Incredibly, however, she did fall into a light slumber that was both dark and dreamless.

A few hours later she came awake with a start, and found Serge crouching beside her, his smoky grey eyes travelling slowly, wonderingly, over her face.

She sat forward, still temporarily

disorientated, then frowned at him.

'What is it?' she asked softly.

He shook his head. 'Nothing. I was just looking at you, that's all. Trying to store up as many memories of you as I can.'

She saw that he was dressed in some of the clothes that had been provided for Korvis, a crisp white shirt, black trousers and a burgundy tie.

'What time is it?' she asked.

'A little after nine.'

Nine! The signing was less than an hour away.

'Lynn,' Serge said gravely, 'I think we should talk.'

'No . . . '

'Yes,' he insisted quietly. 'There are things that have to be said. Things we might not have time to say . . . later.'

Her eyes probed his face, waiting.

'Well . . . I suppose what I want to say most is just thank you. For your compassion, your initiative and your courage. For nursing me back to health and standing by me through everything that's happened over the last few days.'

'Serge — '

He put a finger to her lips, exactly the way he had on Friday night.

'I know this hasn't been easy for you, but you have borne it well, and with a fortitude I can only stand back and admire. You have blessed and inspired me with your bravery, Lynn. And whether you believe me or not, you have awakened something here — ' He reached up to tap his chest. 'Something I have never felt before and will probably never feel again.'

Swallowing hard, Lynn got to her feet and faced him. 'It sounds,' she began, and had to clear her throat before she could continue, 'as if what you're really trying to say is goodbye.'

He shook his head at her. 'What I am really trying to say,' he corrected, 'is that I love you, Lynn. That I will always love you.'

Once again Lynn felt a whirlpool of emotions spinning and warring inside her. When he spoke like this, she could almost believe that it was true, that he really did love her. But . . .

Confused and frustrated, she could only shake her head as she tried to bring order and control to her jumbled feelings. But there were simply too many of them for her to handle.

Suddenly, impulsively, only one thing was right, and she reached for him, went into his embrace, her head tilted back as his came forward, and their lips met in a desperate, passionate kiss through which each was determined to convey all the love and appreciation they would ever be able to muster for the other.

Lips crushing against lips, it went on and on and on, and suddenly the room, the embassy, Ozerov, Miros, Korvis . . . even the city itself simply ceased to be, and for the two fugitives-turned-lovers, all that existed was the joyous feeling they had discovered between them.

At last they broke apart, and Lynn felt Serge's eyes on her but didn't look up. He said, in breathless surprise, 'Well . . . what was that for?'

Coming back down to earth now, Lynn replied guardedly, 'Good luck.'

His fingers kneading her shoulders, he asked, 'Is that all?'

She brought her eyes up to him then, looked him square in the face and saw a longing, a wanting, a needing in him that was the most genuinely real and sincere thing she thought she would ever see in her life. She shook her head and opened her mouth to tell him the truth, but at that moment there was a knock at the door, and they froze in each other's arms.

Serge's eyes shuttled towards the bathroom and he whispered, 'Quick, you'd better get out of sight.'

She made to turn away, then stopped the motion abruptly and whispered, 'Serge . . . '

He looked at her.

Awkwardly she said, 'Be careful. I — I love you, too. With all my heart.'

It seemed as if sunshine filled his

whole countenance then, and quickly she turned and hurried into the bathroom, where she deliberately left a gap in the door that was just wide enough to peer through.

Bending slightly to put one eye to the gap, she saw Serge square his shoulders and reach for his suit jacket. Behind her, Korvis made a sound that was fortunately muffled by his gag, and her immediate, urgent, 'Shhh,' compelled him to further silence.

Outside, Serge opened the door to reveal the conspirators, Ozerov and Miros. Unsmiling now, Miros said, 'It is time, Korvis. Everyone is assembled downstairs. You are ready?'

Trying to match Korvis's much surlier manner, Serge said, 'As ready as I am likely to be.'

Ozerov was studying him with extra care. 'Remember, Korvis,' he said, 'There must be no errors. We are relying on you to carry this thing off, just as you are relying on us for the rewards this performance will bring you.'

'I know what is required of me, don't worry,' Serge replied coolly. 'And from now on, it might be a good idea to use the proper form of address towards me.'

Anger showed on Ozerov's face. 'Don't forget yourself, you insolent — '

But it brought a smile to Miros' otherwise sombre face, and he clapped Serge on the shoulder. 'That's what I like to see,' he commented. 'An actor who really believes in getting into the part.'

Serge stepped out into the corridor and closed the door behind him. Lynn heard the three men walking away and deflated a little. She felt Korvis, bundled unceremoniously into the bath, watching her through wide eyes.

8

She had always known that waiting would be the hardest part of it, of course. But she had never imagined it could be as hard as this.

She paced the room, back and forth, like a caged lioness, trying to convince herself that everything would work out fine, but still that doubting, little voice in her mind kept asking sceptically, 'Will it? Will it?'

She looked up at the clock on the wall. It was nine-twenty. It seemed that time had run at different speeds ever since this affair had started, sometimes faster, sometimes slower. This, she thought bleakly, was one of those occasions when it seemed to drag.

Try as she might, she could not get Serge out of her mind. How was he faring downstairs? He would be mingling with the visiting dignitaries now, prior to the actual signing — or rather, rejection — of the trade agreement. Had Ozerov or Miros already realised that they had the real duke down there now, and not their puppet actor? It was only a matter of time before the deception was uncovered, after all.

If only she could have been there with him . . .

Almost beside herself with worry, Lynn was still pacing the room when she heard footsteps outside. Suddenly she halted, and listened hard.

The footsteps had stopped right outside the room.

A moment later, the doorknob turned and the door itself swung open . . .

Lynn was caught completely by surprise and with no time to hide. All she could do was stare in horror as the door opened wider.

The young maid carrying a change of bed-linen over her arm looked as equally surprised to see Lynn as Lynn was to see her. She opened her mouth to apologise for the intrusion, but something about the girl's appearance sparked off an idea in Lynn's mind, an idea equally as wild and reckless as Serge's had been, but one upon which she decided to act at once.

As casually as she could, she gestured that the girl should come inside, and when she did as she was told, Lynn produced the gun that Serge had left in her care.

With a startled gasp, the maid automatically raised her hands and the clean bed-linen dropped into a heap at her feet.

Taking no pleasure in the fear she saw in the maid's otherwise pleasant face, but accepting that she was involved in an exceptional situation that called for exceptional actions, Lynn said quietly in Russian, 'Don't be alarmed. Although I don't expect you to believe me, I mean you no harm. If only you knew it, we're on the same side.'

Frowning, the maid said, 'Who are

you? What do you want?'

'I haven't got time to explain,' Lynn replied, going over to the wardrobe and taking out a dressing-gown she'd seen there earlier. 'I want your uniform. Now, if you please!'

* * *

Fifteen minutes later, Lynn let herself out of the room and paused a moment in the corridor to smooth the smart, black uniform down across the slim contours of her body. Provided nobody inspected her too closely, she felt reasonably sure she could pass as part of the embassy's staff.

As she walked towards the elevator, carrying the tray and glass that had been delivered the night before to give her disguise an extra touch of authenticity, she felt a pang of regret at having scared the maid, who was, after all, just an innocent bystander in all of this.

Still, she had tried to make the entire encounter painless, if such a thing were possible. Once she had the all-important uniform, she had told the girl to slip into the dressing-gown so that she might preserve her modesty, and had then endeavoured to tie her hand and foot, tightly enough to incapacitate her, but not so tight as to cause her any pain or discomfort.

Silently she promised that she would apologise to the maid again when this was all over. She knew she would get no rest until she did so.

The lift arrived and she stepped inside and pressed the button for the ground floor. Her breathing was coming in short, shallow gasps now, as her nerves began to make themselves felt. A few moments later the lift lurched to a halt and she stepped into a large, high-ceilinged foyer.

Her blue eyes were everywhere at once, so that when she stepped outside, she made directly for the clearly-marked assembly room without hesitation. She passed doormen and security men with barely a glance, and she must have blended in seamlessly, because she encountered no opposition.

Lynn found a spot at the back of the brightly-lit assembly room and looked around. The atmosphere was charged and vibrant. Row upon row of padded velvet chairs, now occupied by officials and businessmen, had been set out facing a long table which stood on a dais up at the far end. Seated at the table were several British politicians whose faces Lynn found familiar, as well as Serge, Ozerov and Miros. Members of the Press were crouching or kneeling before the dais, taking photographs or video pictures, and recording the ceremony for broadcast overseas.

One of the politicians had just concluded a speech to which his audience was giving polite applause. Then Max Ozerov rose slowly to his feet and said into a veritable forest of microphones, 'Ladies and gentlemen, I now give you Duke Serge Varda.'

Another ripple of applause echoed

around the room as Serge got to his feet and nodded graciously. Lynn suddenly felt a rush of pride for this man she loved, this man whom she was now sure loved her, and was glad to be here to witness his moment of triumph.

Clearing his throat, and speaking in careful English for the benefit of his predominantly English-speaking audience, Serge said, 'My friends — for that is what your unstinting generosity and encouragement has made you — we have come here today to sign a covenant that will have far-reaching and beneficial effects for both our countries. In any circumstances, that must surely be a cause for celebration. But before we sign the document, I feel it my duty to sound a word of warning.'

A mumble ran around the room, for this clearly had not been expected, and Ozerov and Miros began to squirm and whisper to each other as they glared up at the man they were only now beginning to identify correctly.

Serge went on, 'This agreement that

binds our countries together has the potential to bring both good and bad. The possibilities for us all are endless and so are the rewards. But it is my view that such agreements, which revolve around trade and commerce, should always be tempered by humanity. We should never forget that inside every factory there is a workforce of sometimes extraordinary men and women, all of whom have hopes and aspirations, just like you and I. These agreements can help them to realise their dreams — if they are fair. But if they reward a privileged few at the expense of the many, what are they really worth?'

Still the large room was filled with the sounds of muttering and shuffling, but Serge paid it no mind and went on in a clear, inspired voice.

'You may wonder at the point I am trying to make. It is simply this. I mentioned possibilities and rewards, but these possibilities and rewards must be there for all.'

Leaning forward, Ozerov hissed behind his hand, 'Sit down, you fool!'

Serge ignored him. 'You good and honourable people may think I am worrying needlessly. Of course you have the good of all at heart, otherwise you would not be here, but I speak now from experience. Experience of what such opportunities can do to twist and corrupt men I would ordinarily have trusted with my life — '

Now Ozerov reached for Serge's sleeve and tried to drag him down, but Serge shook him off and went on, as dogged and determined as ever.

'Yes, I have uncovered a conspiracy that would never have come about but for the greed of a few, easily-corrupted men . . . '

Suddenly his voice dried up and Lynn saw him blink a few times, sway and then reach up to wipe his glistening forehead. Suddenly dread settled heavily in her stomach as she realised that his system was still rebelling against Miros' deadly sedatives.

He slurred, 'I — I refer to these — men . . . '

But Miros had had enough. Springing up, he grabbed Serge and said hurriedly into the microphones, 'Ladies and gentlemen, I must apologise — '

And Ozerov joined him. 'As you can see, the duke is obviously unwell — '

'No!'

All eyes turned to Lynn as she rushed towards the dais, dodging the fumbled attempts of a security guard to catch her.

Serge looked up, frowned, then recognised her and summoned the energy to bark, 'Leave her be! She speaks with my full authority!'

Lynn came to a halt before the long table and pointed first at Ozerov, then Miros. 'These are the men Duke Varda is talking about, these and a small group of others just like them! Men who saw in this agreement an opportunity to line their own pockets, and who then hatched a plan to overthrow the duke, who is a warm and kind man who has only the best interests of his people at heart, and then — to kill him!'

The room was in an uproar now, as men and women rose to their feet and the Press went wild in their frantic attempts to capture it all on film. With desperate expressions now, Ozerov and Miros looked at each other, unsure what to do. But then the matter was settled for them. With a superhuman effort, Serge suddenly shrugged them off and called, 'Guards — arrest these traitors, now!'

All was confusion and struggle after that. The conspirators tried to make a fight of it but were soon placed under arrest. A few of their minions — including Piotr Lanik — tried to escape but were quickly recaptured. Suddenly the audience was pushing forward, eager to hear more details of the duke's remarkable story, but Serge was only interested in one thing.

'Lynn!'

As the crowd pressed in on them, so Lynn and Serge were driven farther and farther apart. Lynn called Serge's name and raised one hand to him. Regaining some of his vitality, he called back, then began to fight his way through the anxious throng, and Lynn followed his example.

Inexorably the two came closer and closer, each whispering the other's name now, arms reaching forward, fingers flexing and questing, nothing else in that room of chaos and excitement mattering now except that each should be reunited, finally and for ever, with the other.

And then they came into each other's arms and hugged and squeezed and laughed and cried, because at last it was all over, and they were alive. It was all over . . .

Surrounded by all the officials and businessmen who had come to witness something far less romantic, though no less important, Serge looked down at Lynn and something deep and loving shifted the smokiness of his grey eyes.

'Did — did you mean it?' he asked.

'What you said earlier?'

Lynn's nod was emphatic.

'Yes, Serge. I mean it.'

'Then will you marry me?'

She hesitated, hardly able to speak for emotion.

'Lynn,' he said throatily, 'every duke should have a duchess. Say yes, I beg of you.'

Wiping tears from her cheeks, smiling now, she said simply, 'Yes.'

A round of applause suddenly exploded from the people gathered around them, and when it died down five minutes later, they went hand in hand back to the dais and Serge finally signed the agreement.

The End.

We do hope that you have enjoyed reading this large print book.

Did you know that all of our titles are available for purchase?

We publish a wide range of high quality large print books including:
Romances, Mysteries, Classics
General Fiction
Non Fiction and Westerns

Special interest titles available in large print are:
The Little Oxford Dictionary
Music Book, Song Book
Hymn Book, Service Book

Also available from us courtesy of Oxford University Press:
Young Readers' Dictionary
(large print edition)
Young Readers' Thesaurus
(large print edition)

For further information or a free brochure, please contact us at:
Ulverscroft Large Print Books Ltd.,
The Green, Bradgate Road, Anstey,
Leicester, LE7 7FU, England.
Tel: (00 44) **0116 236 4325**
Fax: (00 44) **0116 234 0205**

Other titles in the
Linford Romance Library:

LOOKING FOR LOVE

Zelma Falkiner

Fleur's sweetheart, Tom, disappeared after being conscripted into the Army during the Vietnam War. Twenty years later, Fleur finds a package of his unread letters, intercepted and hidden by her widowed mother. From them, she learns that he felt betrayed by her silence. Dismayed, but determined to explain, Fleur engages Lucas, a private investigator, to help in the search that takes them to Vietnam. Will she find Tom there and put right the wrong?

RELUCTANT DESIRE

Kay Gregory

Laura was furious. It was bad enough having to share her home with a stranger for a month — but being forced to live under the same roof as the notorious Adam Veryan . . . His midnight-dark eyes challenged Laura to forget about her fiancé Rodney, and she knew instinctively that Adam would be a dangerous, disruptive presence in her life. She'd be a fool to surrender her heart to such careless custody . . . but could she resist Adam's flirtatious charm?